Burning Bush Bakery

D.L. Barnes

Ocean Time Publishing LLC

Ocean Time Publishing LLC

3760 Sixes Road, Ste 126-114 Canton, Georgia 3011450

Cover photo: difotolife from pixaby/Canva

Cover Design: Canva

Library of Congress Number: 2022913493

ISBN 9798986701950

Chapter 1

"Drew! Are you still there?" asked the female on the other end.

The young man was holding his phone but hadn't responded to the woman's voice for several seconds. Instead, he had been gazing through the window of his luxury mountain home he called his cabin.

The female voice became more intense. "Are you coming over, Drew?" Venessa made the request a second time. She had waited all day for his return and gone ahead planning an evening together.

Drew wanted to push the off button on the phone, but he wanted to be respectful. "I'm tired. I could use some sleep. Could we get together another night?" He rubbed his jaw and felt the scratchiness of stubble on his chin. "I returned home a few hours ago. I was thinking of just going to bed early tonight."

"I was looking forward to us being together this evening."

"Please understand. I don't think I would be good company tonight, and I'd rather get together some other night."

Drew was mentally and physically depleted of energy after the last week. He had barely recovered from the end of the season when he had to fly to Savannah for a week to attend his grandmother's funeral and attend to things that came as a result of her passing.

"You haven't answered me about coming over tonight," Vanessa pleaded.

"I'm very tired. That's all." Drew was distracted by a rainbow that appeared to touch the valley below. Drew interpreted it as a sign from his grandparents. They were in a better place now, reunited with their son, Michael. Drew was becoming more frustrated as he listened to the female's voice on the phone. "I know this sounds cold, but I'd rather spend time alone this weekend. It's been a long couple of weeks since finishing the season last week. Then, I quickly flew to Savanah for my grandmother's funeral. I don't think I would be much company. I hope you understand."

"I understand, but we haven't spent much time together lately. Wouldn't it be nice to have me over to keep you company, Drew? I thought you might like me to fix a salad and put some steaks on the grill. I can pour you a brandy after dinner, and then you can relax the way you like on the balcony. It would be just you and me together for a quiet evening at your home."

Drew moved the handle on the glass sliding door to the balcony and took a few more steps to marvel at the rainbow. "No, I appreciate your offer, but I prefer to be alone this evening and turn in early. I wouldn't be a particularly good listener tonight as my mind is on other things that have happened this week. My conversation skills are exhausted. My body is healing from a tough season of sitting on the bench for the third season. Your other friends would be better companions." Drew could hear the soft sobs that were part of Vanessa's script to coerce what she wanted. "I think I need to go now. It's true that maybe my lifestyle doesn't fit with yours, and that's okay. I'm not going to hold you back from seeing anyone, Vanessa. I feel you deserve to find someone who is committed to the same future. I don't think that is me."

"But, Drew, I do want what you want. I do!"

He heard more sobs through the words. He knew where this was going.

"If you won't let me come over, I'll have to stay here alone this evening worrying about you."

With that, Drew made his last stand. "You have many friends that would enjoy your company. I wish you the best. You'll have more fun without me." Drew heard another sigh over the phone and felt frustration move up to his throat. "Venessa, I need to go. You deserve more than what I have to give. I think that's all I have to say. Good night." He pushed the button to off without another hesitation. He wanted to relax his muscles and mind from the tension of the immediate uncomfortable situation and the accumulated effect from the last week. Drew gave his back and arms a stretch. He hated the negative feeling of disappointing a woman by not giving in to her whims. However, Drew was wise enough to understand that walking away was sometimes the most prudent thing.

Grandfather Robichaud used the word "discernment." With his tinge of Cajun accent, Drew's grandfather explained a similar sticky situation in his colorful way before Drew went to college. The tale began with a man wanting a boat to make a living catching shrimp. Enticed by a swift three sailed stunner that glided through the water faster than any boat, the man almost made a wrong move that would cost him his future happiness. The thrill of the speed and wind at the helm was intoxicating, and he almost succumbed to the temptation of putting his savings into buying the boat. However, the fisherman had been taught discernment as a youth by his wise pawpaw. So, he walked away from the shiny vessel and finally found the one that was just what he needed. The story ended with a slow trawling shrimper's boat, a happy village, and gumbo for everyone on Christmas Eve.

Drew was sure he heard the cleaned-up version of fast cars and women don't always bring happiness that his Uncle Steven warned was coming. Drew gathered his thoughts back to this most recent connection with Vanessa. He liked the reaction from his lady friends when he did something to make them feel special. Unfortunately, Vanessa had a way of taking those gestures and twisting them into an emotional web. It was becoming more evident that she was clawing for a man with the lifestyle she wanted. Her tactics were becoming more apparent. She'd find tasty prey in her sight that met her criteria. The man had to be successful and in a high-profile position. She didn't like to let go until she was ready. She used her little sobs and woeful expressions for her benefit. She'd then devour the morsel and all he had to offer before moving on to the next larger morsel. Drew realized he was being a bit cynical about Vanessa and wanted to stop the hardness that seemed to want to knock on his heart's door. Drew stood for a few more minutes watching the rainbow outside and the sun's illumination on the mountainside. He opened the door to the balcony and took a breath of fresh air to remind himself that all things would work out. He allowed nature's beauty to comfort him from the stress on the inside that had accumulated from the last week. He closed his eyes for a moment and felt a burst of warm air as if it was someone breathing near his ear and a whiff of a beautiful fragrance drifted toward him. It was gone faster than a flicker of light.

Later that night, Drew was still up sitting in his lounge chair, listening to some music, and processing what he was experiencing. He needed a purpose to move forward. Next year would be his fourth year in the pros. It had been his lifelong dream to make it to the professional level. Finally, he made it sort of, at least. He was on a team and loved the game. Now he had a few weeks to heal the body from its war wounds from the season that had just finished with a 23-7 loss. Finally, he was ready to put some time into being Michael Andrew Taylor. He sarcastically laughed to himself. *All these bruises from playing one-quarter of the last game,* Drew thought. *At least I got to play.*

But unfortunately, it happened after the first-string quarterback was injured and unable to return to finish the game in the fourth quarter. *Too bad for Bowman. The bright side was that it got Jack out of a game already in a tough hole at 27-0 which was hard to dig out of with one quarter.*

Drew got the call to finish the last game of the season in the fourth quarter. That described his professional career. The team wasn't rebuilding extremely fast. And it was hard to stay optimistic about the game. He used to pride himself on his athletic and leadership skills. These attributes don't see much success these days. Drew didn't want his mind to go there, but the thoughts sometimes pulled him into a dark place. One small side trip to Savannah to take care of his grandmother's affairs this week, and he was back in his burrow on the side of the mountain, just like bears in winter. In his mind, he would rest up, curled up in his protective habitat behind the gated front entrance of his neighborhood. In the morning, he would rise to the song of birds and mix with the local folk sharing a cold brew after a strenuous mountain bike ride. He didn't have all his life figured out yet. He was sure there was no room in his plan for a smothering, manipulating platinum-blonde female who wanted to put her toothbrush next to his in the bathroom faster than he could wash her white sports car in a brushless car wash. The conversation was the final scene for Vanessa. Drew felt free to cut ties with someone he thought was not part of his future or even felt right in the present.

Around midnight with the gas logs burning, Drew had gotten up and moved to his large desk, reviewing the large pile of documents he had gathered through the week in Savannah. He now had in his possession land in Pennsylvania that had a long-standing tenant. The tenant was willing to buy the property now that Ali Howard had passed. The second property that Drew had more interest in was one on an island off the coast of Georgia near Savannah. It was a small yellow cottage that his grandparents owned and lived in during their married years. He knew this cottage from when he came to visit between breaks at school. He had happy memories of hanging around his father's parents, Charley and Ali Howard. There was never much time to spend with the Howards in Savannah with Drew playing football or practicing in various locations when he was growing up. However, Drew fondly remembered his grandparents coming to many games until he reached high school. He could always find his family out in the stands. His family and close friends wore special hoodies or t-shirts that Grandmother Ali designed to wear on game day. Drew laughed to himself. *It was like having a whole first string on standby in the bleachers.* He remembered the sadness when Grandpa Charley passed. Drew wished he had known more about Reverend Howard. His wife lived happily in the old cottage until she had a stroke two weeks ago. Ali wanted her ashes to be placed with Charley's when she was gone. The request put Charley and Ali next to their son Michael, Drew's father. Michael had died before Drew was born, so his only understanding of his father was what his family told him. If their accounts were correct, Drew was a son of a Roman god, which he doubted. However, Michael was a special person that left this world positively, affecting those who knew him. When Drew's mother stood beside his father's headstone this week and traced his name with her hand, he knew his mother's love had never faded through the years. Drew respected his stepfather, but there would always be a distance between them. It was the bloodline Drew assumed. He did not acknowledge that it went more profound than that. Drew was not ready to investigate his feelings that deeply. He suspected he never would if he had his way.

The time spent with his family this week in Savannah made him think about some things that had impacted him. When he was around fifteen, Drew stopped using the name Papaw for Grandfather Robichaud, his mother's father. Drew thought back and realized it was because he had learned that this man had an influence more significant than within only his family. When Grandfather Robichaud spoke, people responded to him with respect. Drew recalled his grandfather saying, "God gave us a book to guide one through life," when Drew got older and had questions about his future. His grandfather would pull a little black book from his back pocket, and show Drew all the highlighted passages with dates. It still made Drew laugh when he recalled his grandfather's response about a passage scratched out with a black marker.

"I almost screwed up on that one. Thank goodness your grandmother reeled me in fast. I would have missed all her good cooking over the years." He added, "A heavenly light illuminated a thick iron skillet your Grandmother Rona was holding at the time as she contemplated a line drive towards one of my body parts. After that, I never thought of dating anyone else again. I knew she was the only one for me. She still owns that skillet. She insists that it's the secret ingredient to her shrimp etouffee. The truth is that the kitchen skillet is part of her womanly arsenal of wiles, like her favorite fragrance and her little black dress. I loved the whole five-foot-three package since the day we were married!"

Over the years, his grandfather's words came back to Drew. He decided that the story popped back into his mind tonight because of the phone call with Venessa. It was like his grandfather whispering the direction he should take in his ear. Drew enjoyed a quiet evening with a pretty lady. He wasn't opposed to a long-term relationship. Family suited Drew fine, but dating women in search of the right one was a different situation. Drew didn't spend much time thinking about the subject, either. He left that to his mother, CeCe, and Grandmother Reba, who he was sure had confessed some deceptive match-making scheme routinely to Father Petrina since Drew had graduated from college. I could still count on Grandfather Robichaud; he would send warning of any schemes the women in his life plotted against me. Drew laughed to himself. He loved them all, despite all their efforts to influence him.

Turning off the lights in the living room before he went into his bedroom to retire from the long day, Drew looked at the one picture he had of his mother and father celebrating their first anniversary. CeCe and Michael were standing side by side with his father's arm around his mother's waist in front of a watering hole near Savannah. He passed the photo in silence, but his negative thoughts flowed from his head to his heart. His parents had found something that continued to be foreign to him up to this point in his life. *But tomorrow would be a new day to review the game plan of life and search and for that purpose beyond the yard lines.*

In the morning, Drew was flowing through his methodical routine. By the time he reached number 7 on the list, brushing his teeth, he had looked down and saw that a Savannah number had called earlier. Drew sat his brush down and looked at the time. *Who would be texting at 5:45 AM*? He finished his routine list of personal tasks and poured himself a cup of black coffee with no dairy or sugar. He wanted pure stuff. "Don't mess with me before my java takes hold," he would tell the guys. He sifted through a few more messages on his phone. Those messages could wait for now. As he scrolled back up the list of calls, he saw the Savannah number he had seen earlier and opened the screen to read the message.

My name is Phoebe Farmer from the Burning Bush Bakery in Savannah. Please call me about the picture you inquired about at the store this week.

Drew took a few sips of coffee and looked at his watch. The numbers appeared as 7:30 AM. *The bakery would be open, but it would be busy this time of morning he* thought. He decided to work out first and call back mid-morning if he had time. He had left his card with a man on Tuesday at a bakery that he had ordered from while he was on the coast. The Burning Bush Bakery was its name, as Drew recalled. He found it by accident and stopped for coffee one the morning and later ordered something for a gathering after the funeral. During his visit to the local bakery, Drew saw a print on one of the walls of what looked like his grandparents' property. He wanted to know more about the artwork, but the man working referred Drew to contact the bakery owner. Phoebe Farmer must be the owner of the bakery, Drew thought. The number rang a few times when a young feminine voice answered the phone.

"This is Phoebe Farmer speaking."

Drew spoke up. "Miss Farmer, this is Drew Taylor. I am following up on a text you sent me earlier regarding a painting in your bakery. It was the watercolor print"

"Yes, Mr. Taylor, the painting you pointed out belongs to my family."

"Do you know anything about it?"

"Yes, I know a little. Why do you ask?" Phoebe wondered how it grabbed his attention.

"My father's parents lived near Savanah on one of the islands. The painting reminded me of them. It reminds me of the holidays I spent with them on the coast when I was younger."

"I see. Who were your grandparents, Mr. Taylor?" Phoebe asked without giving further information out.

"They were Charles and Ali Howard. My grandfather was Reverend Charles Howard."

"Thank you, Mr. Taylor. I just wanted to know whom I was talking with before sharing any information. I don't remember the Howards having children. But I was born when they were well in their sixties. The painting is from the Howards." Phoebe hadn't lied up to that point, but she was treading on thin ice if she gave more details. "I believe your grandmother painted it. My grandfather and yours were close. Ali gave the painting to my family, and my grandparents cherished it. My mother said that Ali asked that we put the old painting somewhere in the bakery before she died.

My mother may know more. We opened Burning Bush Bakery almost three years ago. Ali had stopped in within the last month before she died and was thrilled to have it shining on the wall. She and I both felt it belonged here. Your grandfather's church was just down the street. I will share with my mother that you asked about the painting. I believe I can speak for her on this matter that the paint is not up for sale. My mother knew Ali well; you may have met my mother at the services. I stayed and covered the bakery while she went."

"Yes, I may have met her among all the people I was introduced to while I was in Savannah. There were mostly longtime family friends, just as my grandmother wanted it. I am terrible at remembering things that aren't

related to football?"

"Football?" Phoebe asked. That caused a stir in her mind. *Was there something she missed that was pertinent to the caller?*

"It's nothing. Please forget I said that. Miss Farmer, would you be willing to sell the painting?"

"I don't think so, Mr. Taylor. It's a family heirloom."

"I understand. I really would make a generous offer if you should be willing to let it go now or in the future. If you ever want to text me a figure at any time, I will consider it and let you know at once."

"Thank you, Mr. Taylor," Phoebe said without elaboration.

Drew was not going to press this time. "Thank you for responding to my request. I might have to come by and admire the painting again and grab a box of those chocolate creamed-filled things."

"Can you tell me more about what you tasted. Did they ooze with sweet white fluffy creme with each bite with a hint of almond flavoring tantalizing covered in a dark rich, moist chocolate cake that you could smell the coca when you unwrapped the wrapper?" Phoebe asked while she was giggling.

"I guess. It looked like a soft chocolate cake, a flying saucer with cream in the center. I think I saw some with red-colored ones too, but I like the brown chocolate ones better."

"That's from an old recipe, most likely of German origins. I was told your grandmother owned an inn there and popularized many local dishes on the menu."

"Fascinating," Drew responded. "I don't know much about either of the backgrounds of my grandparents on my father's side as he passed before I was born."

Phoebe could understand his desire to know more. "Perhaps, if you let me know that you'll be in Savannah, you can drop by the bakery, and we can talk more. Ali Howard influenced several of the items we sell. I add a secret ingredient or two to make it my own. I suppose you've never spent time in Pennsylvania country, have you?"

"No, I've been more west of the Mississippi until recently. However, your explanation reveals why they were excellent. I don't usually eat dairy, sweets, or things with gluten in them, but I would walk several blocks and pass up every pub and coffee shop in between just to have one of those chocolate doodle things you make," Drew teased.

Thank you," Phoebe said.

"Miss Farmer. May I call you Phoebe?"

"Yes."

"I hope we get to meet in person. I will make it a point to stop in the bakery again. Please take my offer seriously. I would be very generous. I would take exceptional care of the painting," Drew said with earnestness in his voice. I will say goodbye, but I look forward to meeting you the next time I'm over on the coast. Thank you for considering my offer."

"Goodbye, Mr. Taylor. It was a pleasure speaking with you." Phoebe thought about his request *interesting phone call* Phoebe thought to herself. Mr. Taylor's request was not something that she could fulfill. Time will show what brought this connection to her life.

♥

Chapter 2

TWO WEEKS LATER, THE night was about to end in a small, renovated cottage that had once served as an officer's quarters on Tybee Island. The alarm from the clock buzzed on the dresser, causing Phoebe to rise from her blissful sleep. She threw her left arm towards the nightstand and shut off the annoying sound. As her left eyelid opened, she could see the full moon's brilliance sending beams through the slats of the window blinds and could make out the number 4:00 AM on the clock. Abruptly, her vision of swimming freely with the dolphins wearing a shimmering silver bikini in a pool of azure blue was plucked from her mind. Phoebe shook her hair out of her eyes and pushed her slender body to a sitting position as graceful as a dance move.

Phoebe's next steps towards the kitchen to start the morning coffee-making ritual alerted her to something foul. She did not expect a wet sensation between her toes as she walked into the confines of her kitchen. But, swishing her feet about in the water as she moved closer to the breakfast bar, she knew something was not right. Phoebe looked around toward the puddling water and scrambled to twist the shut-off valve for the water source leading to the washer. "It's you!" Phoebe sarcastically yelled out as she glared at the black tubing connecting the washer to the wall. She noted the slit that ran down its length, allowing water to flow to the floor freely. Phoebe took a deep breath and thought. *I know God knew this was in my future, so I'm sure He has a plan. It is not the worst thing in the world, but it is enough to start my day off on the wrong wet foot!*

After soaking up the water pooling on the floor and she dried off the tile in the kitchen where the water had spread, Phoebe took a few minutes to make some coffee and take her mug to the porch. There she listened to the roar of the waves rolling in off the Atlantic. The wind carried an icy chill across her cheeks. January was one of the few months of the year that beachfront property might be a lot less comfortable than a cabin with a woodstove blazing in the woods. But, for Phoebe, the sound of waves crashing against the rock barriers at the water's edge was comforting. The rhythm of the water pounding against the rock was a force of nature that needed to be respected. The ocean spoke to those who would listen and alert land dwellers of peace or peril coming by sea. She sipped a few more mouthfuls of her mocha latte as she watched the waves roll in before finishing a quick spritz of water on her face and grabbing a change of clothes. Soon she was driving over the bridge that brought her to the mainland and onto the streets leading to the bakery.

Fifteen minutes later, Phoebe heard voices coming in through the service door opening off the alley. She felt a little relief knowing that she wasn't alone in a building that was still deserted this time of the morning.

Jesse looked at the typically perfectly coiffed female in front of him and knew an unraveling disaster had happened somewhere. The mastermind of the kitchen madness was already laying out the pans and ingredients that made up the symphony of the morning routine before the bakery opened. Sun-kissed strands of silky hair cascaded past each naked earlobe, and a simple band held the ponytail in the back. Phoebe was out front wiping down the glass cases that displayed the pastries and cakes to the customers. Her uncle affectionately gave the five-foot, six-inch strawberry blonde female the nickname "Mermaid". The diminutive violet-eyed niece was hard at work, finishing the items on the list of things to do before opening at 7:00 AM when Jesse arrived.

"Seems to me, Phoebe, you look rough around the gills this morning," Jesse commented as he came from the back room into the storefront area.

"Oh, be still. I wrestled with a water hose this morning and rushed around cleaning the mess up. I'm leaving to meet the repairman at eleven. So why bother with makeup this morning? Besides, my mother will be in before I need to leave. She can do everything I can do."

"Not that I care, but your prince from some far-off kingdom might come through that door today, and you're looking like, shall I say… a bit like you've been riding in a storm on a motorless bristle contraption with a wart growing on that pretty nose. If I start hearing you start cackling, I know my assumption is true that the sea creature has kidnapped my sweet mermaid and transformed her into this creature of Haute de monster."

"Oh please, Jesse!" Phoebe tried to look perturbed. *I*t was often hard not to smile when Jesse used his wit to say something. "Besides unconditional love, right? That's what you always say! He will love me, warts and all, right?"

"You got me on that one, sugar. I dare say no more, or I shall be banned from this establishment."

Phoebe rolled her eyes. "Jesse, why do I try to talk sense to you? Oh yeah! I remember you are my mother's brother, and we share the same gene pool. I was doomed from birth!"

"You be careful around your elder's smarty pants. Your family was so proud of you when you finished college at that expensive private college in Maine, and this is the love we get when you return. Okay, Mermaid, you'll see who's got your back!"

"Uncle Jesse, I love you just the way you are!" Phoebe said, giggling.

"That's better. Now the day feels right." Jesse looked up through his glasses and poured himself coffee from the fresh pot. "Let's get this day started." He smiled back with a twinkle in his eye.

The early morning regulars came and went. Phoebe settled into her morning routine, and soon the clock was approaching 9:30 AM. The morning crowd had slowed down to a steady pace. Phoebe turned the ropes over to Jesse and the assistant, so she completed work in the back office before her mother showed up. She even made a couple of calls. Finally, her mother popped in just shy of 10:00. Phoebe was now free to leave and wrestle with the watery issue awaiting her at home. She put an envelope in the outgoing mailbox, stopped at the counter to put a croissant in box, and grabbed an unsweetened tea. Phoebe was ready to leave and saw a red Italian sports car pull in on the other side of the street. Her face began to lighten up, and then she remembered. Today she ran out of the house with her hair pulled back and no makeup. "Oh, no!" Phoebe blurted out. The man driving the redeye candy was jaywalking in the bakery's direction.

Jesse announced his arrival as he looked through the kitchen door window. "Rock Muffin coming up starboard," he said in Phoebe's direction. Jesse made a fast move to reduce a direct collision with the fast-moving female. He raised his eyebrows as she passed by, nearly bringing down the tray of quiches that Jesse was holding. He smiled as he peeked behind him and saw her take out the pink lipstick from her pocket. She disappeared behind a closed door. He looked over at Phoebe's mother and said, "She learned that step in one of those ballet classes she took growing up. It looked like a pirouette to me." Jesse threw Darla a grin and shrugged his shoulders.

Darla looked up and let her eye gaze at the parking meters on the other side of the street. She then looked at Jesse and teasingly scolded him. "Oh, Jesse, let her be. She thinks she must look her best when you know who comes in the door. I think he's smitten already, if you ask me. He could send anyone to pick up his order. Yet, he somehow always comes in the morning that she's here. There's a reason he stops in when he does. Besides, he's a sweet customer. I think it's romantic to watch the little flirtation when he comes in."

Just then, the bakery door opened, and all eyes behind the counter returned to their tasks. A young man wearing jeans with an expensive buckle and a white shirt came walking closer to the counter. His dark sunglasses concealed his eyes, but his facial expression showed warmth.

Phoebe came from the back just in time to give a bright smile to everyone and offer her help.

"Hello, sunshine," the man said, standing at the counter and looking at Phoebe. He pointed to the tall cup on the counter. I missed your fresh tea. But, iced or hot, it's still the best."

"Nice try, but you know the grower is just up the road an hour or so, and you can get there all year around. For you, they would brew on demand as soon as you arrived." Phoebe's eyes tried to stay focused on the items on the shelves, but she felt her cheeks heating up.

"Well, yes, but there's something about drinking it with a fresh muffin that I know is your specialty and so healthy for me. Isn't that what you always tell me when I come in to visit the bakery?" the customer said with a teasing tone to his voice.

"Yes, I must confess. I am guilty of that," Phoebe responded with her prettiest smile, her eyes lighting up with merriment.

"It's been a couple of months since you've been in the bakery. So, I assumed you were out of town."

"Yes, I was in Nashville writing and went to the west coast to do some videos with the band. Now, I'm back for a few weeks and will be back on the road later in February. Ice storms in the past have been an issue in January for the last couple of years, so management wanted to start the tour in February to reduce snafus.

Phoebe looked up with a questioning expression.

"It's all okay. We all needed to rest as we worked through New Year's Day this year. Can you throw in half a dozen of your submarine-looking loaves there? I have friends coming over, and I think those rolls would be great with some shrimp on the grill. Don't forget my blueberry swirl with

cinnamon."

Phoebe's mind was momentarily lost in a memorizing daydream, neglecting to see others who had come and gone into the shop, until a stranger's voice approached the counter to her left. The voice was commanding and deep, but warm and soothing, like drinking a hot tea with cream and honey on a cool, windy morning on the shore. The tall and well-built young man selected something and handed it to the other assistant behind the counter.

The man asked, "Is Miss Farmer in the store today?"

Phoebe looked away for a moment, but did not verbally respond. She finished collecting the items for her patron and neatly packed them in a handled shopping bag. The bakery's owner wanted to tell him that his music made her want to dance in the wind. A secret desire like that would have been too revealing. However, she felt static in her fingertips and quickly moved her hand back. Questioning, she looked up and around the room. Again. She heard someone mention her name and finally shot a glance at the unknown customer.

Jesse looked up from his business of refilling the bread baskets with some freshly made sourdough and walnut cranberry loaves. He let the assistant take the next customer and responded to the man. "Hello, you're the gentleman asking about the painting?"

"Yes, that was me a month ago. I was wondering if the owner or Ms. Farmer was here today. I spoke with her over the phone."

"Yes, Miss. Farmer hasn't left yet." Jesse looked over at the end of the counter. "Phoebe, why don't you come over and introduce yourself in person," Jesse said with a voice that directed Phoebe to come closer.

She pulled her lips together for a moment and pushed her chin up as she walked over to the tall man with blue eyes and a clean-shaven jawline. She scolded herself for noticing the handsome face.

"Hello, I'm Phoebe Farmer."

"Miss Farmer, I am Drew Taylor. I spoke with you over the phone about the painting on your wall. So, I thought I would come by again when I was in town."

"Hello, Mr. Taylor."

"Please call me Drew," he said with a smile.

Phoebe stammered. "I-I am pleased to meet you, Mr. Howard." She then ducked her chin for a minute and tugged on her ponytail out of nervousness. "My mother is here today, and you can ask her in person, but I believe she will give you the same answer. Let me get her."

Jesse spoke up. "Let me get Darla, and you can take Mr. Taylor to our private sitting area; I will bring you some tea. Do you like your tea, sweet Mr. Howard?"

"Yes, I do, but you don't need to bother."

"It's not a bother, sir. This way, Phoebe and her mother can talk about your interest in stopping in. We are just family here." Jesse said, with pure mischief in his eyes.

Phoebe had seen that look before. This time, she was the target of his mischief. She pinched her nose up at her uncle while the stranger's back was toward the direction of the archway to the other room. "Yes, Drew, please follow me, and mother can join us," Phoebe said ever so politely as she felt prickly sparks down her spine."

"Are you here on vacation?" Phoebe asked, trying to fill the silence. "There is some great golf course in the area."

"I have some friends in the area right now and might meet them tomorrow, but my purpose today is to check on my grandparents' home. I am thinking of keeping it. It has sentimental value to me."

"Yes, I understand that. It is a lovely place. It's on one of the quieter islands." Phoebe perked with interest and continued excitedly, "There's a little local market to get basic staples, so there's no need to drive to the mainland. I don't live on the same island, but I love that location, even just driving by. The cottage has always been a charmer on that street. I never want it to fall into disrepair on being unloved." Phoebe felt herself blush.

"Well, that says something of value about the property," Drew responded stoically.

Embarrassed at sharing something personal with this stranger, Phoebe took a moment of silence but quickly perked back up again as she saw her mother coming through the French doors. "Here's my mother now."

"Drew Taylor, I am so happy to see you again. We met at your grandmother's service. Jesse gave me these drinks. I know my daughter takes her tea straight, so I assume I have the sweet tea right here, Drew. It's a perfect ratio of sugar, tea, and steeping time. I have your grandmother's recipe. My father liked it this way, but he would occasionally like his scotch on the rocks before bedtime. Just a family secret." Darla did not look like her daughter except for her eyes, which must be a genetic trait in the family.

"So that's what makes your tea different than the rest. I promise I won't say a word about it," Drew responded with a warm smile.

Darla continued with the conversation. "So, Drew, will we enjoy having you here now that you own Charley's and Ali's home?"

"I am investigating the possibility of spending more time here. I need to be in Atlanta for most of the year, but outside of that, many of my colleagues have homes elsewhere." Drew was trying to be coy by not giving out too much information.

Phoebe's mother was looking at him with probing eyes as if she was reading a message that wasn't in the physical world. "Yes, I think you will like it here very much."

Drew wasn't sure he could hide his cards from this woman during a poker game. He wished he had this woman with him last Friday when he lost $500.00 in a game at a barbeque at J.C.'s house. But instead, Drew's eyes turned back to Phoebe, who smiled back sweetly, but then looked at her watch.

"Mama, Drew asked about the painting on the wall, and I told him we were not willing to sell the painting. I didn't think your opinion would be different from mine, but I will let you have your say. In the meantime, I am going to excuse myself. I must meet a repair person at my place in a short while. I am glad to meet you in person, and I hope we see more of you. My mother can share information about your family and the painting with you, as I would not have much to offer."

Drew stood up and allowed Phoebe to walk by the exit. He hid his disappointment that the young woman was leaving the conversation. He looked at her with seeking eyes. "I don't think that's true. From what you told me over the phone, there's a lot you can share with me. You have the history of being here where my grandparents lived. There are people here who knew my father when he was alive. That is a part of my life that I am sadly missing." He looked serious for a moment. "I hope to spend more time with and learn more about my grandparents."

Phoebe was taken aback for a second but responded affirmatively. "Yes, I will make myself available. You have my number." She bowed her head, tugged her ponytail, and dashed out the door. The visitor strangely seemed a part of her past and present. Her heart raced unexpectedly. She wrestled with the thoughts flooding into her mind and heard the voice of cynicism. *He is just one of those trophy collectors. He holds his treasure for a moment and puts it on the shelf, the wall, or worse yet, a closet where no one ever sees the piece of art again."* Phoebe raced outside to catch another glimpse of her musician friend driving away a couple of blocks up the busy street. She was able to make a friendly gesture as she saw him look her way as he made the left turn at the light. She was loyal to keeping his name private, as he had kept her secret safe. Phoebe groaned to herself. "Well, maybe next time."

In the meantime, Drew had parted ways with Phoebe's mother and exited the bakery. He returned to his car.

Phoebe had another responsibility to attend to, and so was in a hurry. As she pulled around the corner of the shop to the adjoining parking lot, she passed a white convertible with Italian leather—a nice car. Phoebe wondered for a moment before she pulled out of the lot and glanced in her review mirror. *So, who are you, Drew Taylor? Did the whisper in the wind bring you here?*

Several hours later, and with a few dollars less in her checking account, Phoebe turned into the parking lot of a local eatery on the island where she lived. She entered the door, and a loud greeting met her from the bar. "Well, look here. Sunshine came in to see me this week!"

"Oh, Myles, you are always a pleasure. Do you think I could have a tall, iced coffee? I'm going to sit out on the back screened porch section. I came early before the evening crowd. By the way, have you been hanging out with Rock Muffin?" she teased.

"You got it. Hey, your twin is next door, estimating me. Rock Muffin has been in to see me just the other day. He always asks if I have seen you and how you're doing."

Phoebe smiled, "That's nice. I saw Danny's truck. Tell him I will buy him dinner if he joins me."

"I will. If Danny doesn't accept, I will pour one of my tall necks and take my break, enjoying the company. Now here you go. When I saw you pull in, I poured the brew over the ice in the hurricane glass."

"Thanks, Myles."

"I'm a sucker for your smile," Myles responded.

Phoebe giggled as she grabbed the glass and napkin. "I'll be out there." Phoebe had changed from the morning at the bakery and felt more like herself.

Myles finished wiping the counter and grabbed his phone to tell Danny his sister was waiting. A minute later, Myles's phone blew up with Danny's message.

Myles smiled and responded, pushing in the letters. Ready in five.

Phoebe sat with thoughts running through her head. A white egret came to stand near the side of the screened deck. After a few minutes, she saw Danny walk towards her from the property next door

"What's the special occasion?" Danny asked as he approached the table.

"Mom sent me to check up on you," Phoebe teased. "No, I just wanted to relax after a crazy day, and I saw the truck. Phoebe looked pensive. "I owe you dinner after putting up the new light fixtures outside the bakery."

"Not really, but I will take that as an opportunity to have one of Myles's great sea creations and sit for a moment." Danny saw the restaurant owner walking toward the table with food in hand. "Shelly's away tonight."

Myles interrupted the conversation. "Danny, I prepared the island's finest for you, and it's in my hands. If you need anything, let me know. I'm going back in and prep for the night crowd."

"Thank you, Myles." She gave him a wink.

Danny began to organize everything on the table. "You're a good man!"

Myles wiped his hands on the towel on his belt. "You got that right. I'll check on you in a few minutes."

Danny moved the extra plate in front of his sister and poured half of the deep-fried golden globes on her scale along with half of his sandwich. "He took one big bite of the grouper po'boy. "This is so good!" It tastes like our buns, are they?"

"I suppose so. It looks like the ones we make at the bakery. Here, take this napkin. You have sauce on your chin."

Danny looked at Phoebe to confirm that he had removed it. "What's going on in your world today? Are you on one of those missions to save another sea turtle, or did you come to share another of your stories of ghosts you're always telling?" Danny took another bite while he waited for Phoebe to fire off one of her snarly remarks as part of the fun of spending time with your sibling.

"You're being ugly. The customers love my ghost stories, and the sea turtles are a gift of nature that we need to protect." Phoebe grinned back at her brother. "I was going to tell you that Rock Muffin is back in town. But, of course, I looked like a chimney sweeper who had just finished cleaning every rowhouse chimney in the historical district! He said he was off the tour for a while." Danny looked up and touched his nose showing Phoebe that she had a speck of something sitting on the tip. "It's nice having him return to the shop. That means he likes coming in. He is a nice guy." Drew took another bite of his po'boy and savored the taste of fresh grouper mixed with spicy sauce and Myles's unique coleslaw mix. In Drew's opinion, it was the best around. "Do you two ever talk about anything more than the muffins?" He looked over at Phoebe and gave her a big smile. Danny enjoyed teasing his sister about the guy she nicknamed Rock Muffin.

Rock Muffin had an affinity with the family that began about three years ago. Unexpectedly, he showed up at the bakery shortly after it opened. It was a surprise but not an unwelcome shock. Orders frequently came from households in the same affluent gated neighborhood where Rock Muffin lived. Typically, those customers had specific arrangements for delivery or pickup. But instead, Rock Muffin came in person to make his purchase. The Celtic troubadour asked Phoebe what her favorite muffin was in the pastry case. She let him have a nibble of the blueberry cinnamon swirl and agreed. It's been his favorite. After that, whenever he stopped in the bakery, he never forgot to request at least one blueberry swirl with a pinch of cinnamon.

"Stop!" Phoebe snapped back to her twin. "I try to converse with him when he comes in the shop. I don't have much in common with a musician who tours the country in motor homes and planes."

"That's not true. You have all that classical dance training and musical background. You would understand the guy's industry more than most."

"Yes, in the past. Now, I'm just a baker behind a counter of French pastries, special loaves of bread, and sugary treats. The sugar and nothing more drew in him."

"He keeps coming in, though, and that says something. There's something in the bakery that he likes. He could send somebody for it or arrange delivery."

"That's what mother says too. I'm just waiting for him to make an invitation. He is just shy. Anyway, change of topic. Somebody else came in today. I thought it was interesting."

Danny took some chilled tea from his glass. "Who was that?"

"Do you remember Reverend Howard and his wife having a son?"

"The son, I don't remember. I recall that there had been a fatal car accident many years ago. It was before you or me. Why do you ask? Was that one of your ghosts you saw in the store today?"

"No, you are being bad again," Phoebe huffed. "It was the grandson of Revered Howard, who has grown up and is about our age. He must be doing well as he drives an expensive car and offered to pay well for a painting in the bakery."

Drew stopped mid-reach for a hush puppy to say, "I remember him vaguely as a young boy when he would visit the Howards. Grandpa would ask me to come along fishing or scrounging around for oysters when he was here. He was born after his father died. His mother must have been expecting him when the accident happened. He was a surprise blessing to the family, from my recollection. The Howards made over him so much that it almost made me nauseous. Charley and Grandpa would take us out on the boat for an afternoon. Sometimes Drew's Grandfather came with him on the plane when he was young.

"Why didn't you ask me to come when you were scrounging in that oyster muck?" Phoebe looked up, teasing with her perturbed look and pouting lips. She then continued sipping on her iced coffee.

"You were a girl and always spent time in your ballet lessons or musical recitals. But, lucky for Mom and Dad, you didn't enjoy the joys of shopping till you hit your teens." Danny said.

"By then, you started hanging around Margie. So, we went on different

paths at that point."

"I think I'm detecting a powerful spirit of cynicism." Phoebe scrunched her nose as she did when she was teasing sarcastically. "I just want you to know I would have had fun with you all in the muck and that messy fun stuff you, Dad, and the rest of your friends always got into."

"Yeah, but Dad was just as bad as me for finding wild adventures. I wasn't old when I last saw Charley's grandson. Charley passed away when we were in high school. I don't think I saw Drew much after that. His mother remarried. That's all I know."

"His name is Michael Andrew Taylor, not Howard. He told me clearly over the phone when he first called and asked me about the painting. He saw the painting on the wall when he showed up at the bakery to pay for an order someone had placed while he was here for his grandmother's funeral."

"Strong name," Danny replied. "I remember calling him Andy. Andy makes me think of red hair and freckles. He most likely feared being teased about that as a kid, so he went for Drew instead. Is he just visiting, or is he in town overseeing his grandmother's business? She was a successful woman in her own right. I'm sure she had some financial holdings left to him."

"Perhaps, I remember him saying he was thinking of keeping the home where his grandfather lived. That was one thing he inherited."

"It's on a nice lot, and the home is of excellent construction. It has a lot of customized features that Charley did himself. He was a natural artist. I would keep the cottage, too, if a person left it to me. I would consider buying it if it ever went on the market. It's too small for a large family, though. Why the interest in the details?"

"I don't know exactly. I didn't put too much thought into thinking about Howard's grandson today." Phoebe bit her lip afterward, hoping Danny had not heard the slight fib. "I left him with mother as I had an appointment with the plumber who had to fix a hose from the washer. I was not looking quite the southern beauty at the time after sweeping up an inch of water off the kitchen when I woke up this morning."

"Yuck! I assume it's now fixed?"

"Oh yes!" Phoebe switched the topic back. "I'm just wondering what mother decided about the painting. He didn't leave with it, but I don't think mother would keep it from him if he wanted it. She is wiser than I am. If there's a reason that she's holding on to the painting, then I agree."

"I'm sure we will find out her rationale, and I suspect we will see this person again if he is Drew Taylor."

Just then, Myles came out with a pitcher of iced tea. "Just thought I would come out and top you off. Is there anything I can get you?"

"No, you know me, Myles," Phoebe said back with a twinkle in her eye. "I'm one drink a night, girl. Otherwise, I start dancing on tables."

Myles teased back. "I was hoping you would say that. I've been trying to encourage that for some time now! So, you tell me when and I will start pouring the second drink of your choice."

Phoebe twitched her nose. "Myles, are you picking on me too? I thought I could trust you to watch my back!"

"Never, kiddo, but Danny here would surely knock my lights out if I didn't stop your tab when you got a little crazy. If that didn't persuade me, he'd bring the backhoe and make his point clear enough," Myles said with good humor.

Danny shook his head and made a facial expression, as if he agreed with that statement. "Hey, maybe you know more information? Myles, does a Michael Andrew Taylor or a Drew Taylor ring any bells for you?" Danny asked. "You are knowledgeable of all things important."

Myles paused, thinking for a moment. "Yes, it does," Myles said, keeping busy picking up the dirtied plates.

"Well?" Phoebe asked, surprised that Myles could make a connection so fast.

"Who is he?" Danny asked.

Myles looked at them both with a sly grin. "He has some friends around here."

Danny looked at Myles with questioning eyes. "You know more. Let me know what you know, or the estimate I was going to do will go up another $500 before I leave this porch!"

Myles bantered back. "Danny, I never thought of you as an extortionist!" He then answered the questions with some bits of information that he knew. "What's to know? Nice guy, just a little more guarded than some. He plays a sport called football. I know you are not a game watcher, but some people are. There are several professional players in the area that he hangs out with when he's in town. He's a different sort than what I knew of his grandfather. Everybody knew Charley. I can't think that he had one enemy. Although I'm sure there were some around town. From my understanding, Reverend Howard raddled a few birds from their perches in his lifetime. But that's old information. I will tell you that Drew Taylor has played professionally now for about the last three or four years. He's not the first stringer, though, but he should be. The guy has the talent, from what I know of his background. He's missing that magic, I guess. Drew is a smart player, not just a jock. He's got connections in the sport and outside of the sport. I don't have a lot more to say. He's been here a few times with friends. I helped with catering a poker game at one of his friend's places. It was at a home where some rockers and professional players live. They circle in that same stratosphere. I sense he is very much a gentleman. I didn't see him drink a lot when I ran into him. I remember that for a reason. Taylor mixes well with the guests at parties. He gave me the impression that he was accustomed to being around the high achieving crowd. He knew all the social graces that go with the scene. The guy has a waiting list of females who would be happy to be his chief interest. Is that all you need to know?"

"That's fine. Myles, you've done your fiduciary duty to my sister here, who had an earlier encounter with him today," Danny said. He then looked over the table at Phoebe.

Myles added, “I hoped that helped you. I haven’t seen him often, but I have seen him around over the last three years, especially in the off-season. He had family here, and his grandmother, Mrs. Howard, may have needed him to manage some of her business interests. He was the only grandson.”

“Drew Taylor stopped by the bakery today, Myles,” Phoebe said. “I also spoke with him a few weeks ago about a painting he saw.”

“Well, mermaid, it seems like he’s caught your attention. You rarely show much interest,” Myles responded. Myles looked at Danny. “He may be a sea turtle as he hides in his shell, the kind Phoebe likes to save. But he's not the soft-shell kind. He will come out snapping when he feels the need to protect.” Myles raised his eyebrows and said no more.

“Mermaid?” Danny scoffed at Myles's remark. “Well, that confirms that Uncle Jesse has been here too much and has become an influence. I’m not sure that’s good or bad, but he does can rub off on people.”

Myles nodded and laughed. “He’s a fine man!”

Phoebe’s mind was still on the visitor today. She felt a sense of compassion for Charley’s grandson after hearing more information about him and felt a pang of pain for his loss of his father without ever knowing him. “I think he’s looking for something. He doesn’t understand it yet, but I sense that he is empty and looking for what Charley found after he became sober. It’s the same thing that called Drew Taylor here. It’s what Ali put her faith in all those years.”

Myles shrugged his shoulders. "The coastal breezes have that effect on some people. Whoever works in the bakery's kitchen has been calling him back. Jesse has a deeply craggy mug from his days on the shrimp boat. I suspect it's not him."

"Or a private golf club and the local microbrewery," Danny added before draining his glass. "I say we settle the check so I can run home and get into my off-hours attire."

"What attire is that? You have seven t-shirts, one for each day of the week, and matching joggers when you are not in your white shirt and tan slacks for business."

"That's what I mean. I'm out of sorts when I'm not back in my real skin before sunset. I have somewhere to be this evening, so I appreciate the fine dining experience with my sister, who's picking up the tab." Danny smiled in Phoebe's direction.

"It's on me. I owed you one for the help this week," Phoebe said.

"Yes, you did. But unfortunately, my short-term memory is weak, and I can't remember what perils I saved you from this time," Danny teased. I'm going to be sure the next tab will be higher."

Myles was comfortable with the banter between siblings, so he knew not to interfere. He assumed It was all part of their bonding in the womb.

"Myles, I will email you the estimate in the morning. It shouldn't be an extensive project. I think it's an innovative idea."

“Thank you. That sounds good to me. Phoebe, you stop even without that rascal. I’ve always got one ready on tap for you. Hey, I also wanted to tell you that those rolls we’ve been getting from your bakery for the po’boys are a smash with the customers.”

Drew looked at Phoebe and winked when he heard Myles' confession. He nodded his head in agreement.

“It has increased my call in orders since we changed to those rolls from your bakery. Nothing is better than your fresh rolls with a little of my secret sauce and seasonings on the fresh grouper and shrimp coming in off the boat. Add a tall glass of one’s choice, and we are talking about fine dining in flip-flops. We may not do it as they make them in Louisiana, but I’ve got my twist that rivals the best of them. The customer always knows when there is a little love from the oven.” Myles gave a wink in Phoebe’s direction.

“Thanks, I’ll tell Uncle Jesse. It was his recipe. He loved the taste challenge part while we were creating the right shape and blend of ingredients to make the crust perfect on the outside. He is still perfecting the beer bread made with one of the local microbreweries. I’m not sure if he has yet gotten past the right liquid ratio, " Phoebe joked.

“Jesse’s one of a kind.” Myles laughed. “Every family has one of those in their family tree. You love them but don’t know what to do with them when they are around. You learn to accept them and be who they are.”

"Yes!" Danny and Phoebe both agreed and started for the door. Finally, they made it to their vehicles, shaded by the old shade trees that still graced the area despite new storefronts and merchants arriving.

Phoebe's eyes were drawn to the other end of the parking lot in front of the barn that housed the local market. A sporty convertible was parked outside. "Hey, look!" Phoebe tilted her head towards an imported sports car parked in front of the market. "It's his car!"

Danny looked around at the assortment of cars parked in the area. "Who's the car?" "Taylor's!" Phoebe added an exaggerated movement of throwing a football with her hand. "Do you want to meet him?"

Danny shrugged his shoulders. A few seconds later, the man in question walked out of the store with a grocery bag full of items.

Phoebe greeted the man she had met earlier in the day. Dark wavey hair, brown eyes, and a body that was fit from toenail to ear lobe. What was it in the description she did not provide to Danny? Phoebe's heart pricked into her thoughts like a thorn. She wanted to be honest, but didn't want to reveal too much.

Danny looked over at Phoebe with an innocent expression, as if he was not taking the bait. "Was there something you needed to add, Phoebe?" Danny knew his sister and the effects of her charm.

"No, thank you!" She turned her head back and smiled.

Drew freed his hands from the bundle and closed the trunk.

Phoebe looked around and spoke the first words. "Hello, Drew. It's nice to run into you again."

Drew looked up to see who had greeted him. When he saw who I was, his facial expression softened.

"I live near here, and my brother and I were just hanging out next door," said Phoebe. "Let me introduce you to someone I think you might have met in the past?"

"Sure," Drew said with a slight grin, accepting the offer.

"Danny, this is Mr. Drew Taylor, Reverend Howard's grandson," Phoebe said to her brother, while Danny greeted the male standing across from him.

Danny presented a firm handshake and a smile to the newcomer. "My grandfather and yours were neighbors. We met when you came to visit as kids."

Drew took a few moments to think back. "Yes, I remember you," Drew spoke with warmth and guardedness. "It's nice to visit the area and run into an old acquaintance." Drew looked at both, recognizing their similarities and realizing they must be twins. He suspected they were identical twins. "I planned to stop by this little place and stock up on my supplies for a few days. I got lucky and found what I was hoping to find." Drew didn't elaborate.

Phoebe wondered if he had passed this way many times before. She continued to smile, observing his responses through her designer sunglasses. Phoebe presented herself with high southern charm, but kept her true thoughts to herself.

Danny spoke, "Phoebe mentioned you were thinking about taking over the Reverend Howard's home on this island. It's a desirable location, and the house has some notable features. I also know that if you would like to sell it, realtors would drool at the opportunity to list it. I don't know how it fits with your life now, but that house has a heart you don't find in many other places—excellent building materials in that house. That is one of a kind. You've been there, so you know what is there."

"Yes, I feel more like I will keep the property for myself, but I can't live here full time. I need to be near a certain location, at least for part of the year." Drew looked at Phoebe. "I hear you are incredible with ghost stories. Are there any stories about the cottage?"

"Oh no, did my mother tell you that? There are only happy memories there." She smiled back, blushing as she could feel her cheeks heat up. "I can tell stories of pirates' remorse and souls reunited with loved ones along the coast. The story parts are mostly true—the ghost comes from tales that keep coming back generation after generation. My favorite stories are the ones that talk about something calling the person to be somewhere at the right time or the right place. Without hearing the call, the characters would have missed their destiny in life."

"I think I have grown old and cynical for the likes of fairies, mermaids, and such," responded Drew.

Phoebe said with a sudden feeling of sadness. "I wish everyone could love the stories as I do."

"I see. Well, you can share some with me, especially those of lost sailors and shipwrecks off the coast. I do enjoy a good salty sailor in peril." Drew said with a smile.

Phoebe smiled back, not wanting to provide an opinion. She knew he didn't know her well enough to trust her openness. Hopefully, another time would bring them together to dive into a more fruitful conversation. "Yes, we don't want to take up too much of your time, Drew. We just wanted to say hello. We are glad to have you in the area for as long as you wish to stay."

Drew looked into Phoebe's violet eyes for a moment and then quickly turned his head away. He found this little frame of flex colored hair and fair skin bronzed by a natural glow from the sun quite attention getting. I must pull away, he thought. "Danny, do you play golf?" Drew asked, turning back to the other member of the triad.

"Sometimes, I'm probably not at your league, but I occasionally play a round," Danny responded.

"I suspect that's not true, but we'll see if we can't arrange something. Do you have a business card so I can leave you my contact information?"

"Yes, sure. Here it is. My cell is right here." Danny scribbled down a number on the back. "The other contacts go through the office first, but you can reach me through this number. Of course, the office can always reach me if I don't return your call immediately."

"Thank you. I will call you and will work something out. Do weekends work best? Are you off during the week for a game of golf?"

"I run my own business with men working for me. I can cut out sometime."

"Great! Let me settle in first and get some things taken care of, and I will be in touch," Drew responded, moving to open the door. "Phoebe, I would like to get to know you more, too. How does a day jog on the beach sound? I think sunset runs are better for you with your schedule. We could stop and relax afterward and talk about the island. Your mother warned me about your Uncle Jesse, living right next door in your grandparents' house. He sounds like a lot of fun!"

"Yeah, he's a barrel of a hot mess! That's not an exaggeration. Drew said his goodbyes and started moving toward his vehicle.

Phoebe would have liked to have spent a few more minutes talking, but it was time for her to continue her day. "Goodbye again, Drew."

"Thank you, Phoebe. I may very well be here for several weeks this time," Drew said before moving closer to his car door. "I'll be talking with you again."

The siblings pulled out behind the white foreign convertible and followed until they each needed to peel off the main highway to their destinations. Drew rushed back across the causeway, yearning to explore the nooks and crannies of the cottage on the marsh.

Chapter 3

IT HAD BEEN THREE weeks since Drew took the cottage over. He was surprised at how little he had to do to be right at home. The area above the garage suited him fine, and with a few changes in furniture to better fit his lanky legs, he was quite comfortable. From a distance, he could hear sounds of the low country, if not the sea itself, especially late at night when he left the windows partially open in the loft. He found the lane he lived on was perfect for a jog to awaken his mind and body in the morning. During the early evenings, he could use that time to relax and get away from phones, emails, and other disturbances that carried his mind from more important things in life. Something was soothing about being around the twins, too. Danny and Phoebe had become quite a positive influence. Their Uncle Jesse had his pleasant uniqueness, too. Drew smiled in amusement, thinking of the middle-aged distiller next door who tinkered with his home brews at his leisure. Danny joked about his uncle. He couldn't reveal much about Jesse as he was in a secretive protection plan and not part of the Farmer tribe. Drew might believe that except for the violet eyes and flex colored blond hair, that was distinctively a family trait in the Farmer siblings. Drew would not deny that the flock came from the same species, unique and exasperating as that could be. He took a deep breath as he made it for the last quarter of a mile before turning left at the mailbox. After this week, there would be no more business outings where Danny would take Drew off to a project that needed some ideas regarding equipment. With Drew's connections with his Grandfather Robichaud and Uncle Steven in Louisiana, electricity flowed between the group and the workers involved on the sites. There was pride in finishing the open shopping plaza on the main street of that small town where the peach painted on the water tower had been a land marker for years. It wasn't just a job for many older guys who'd been around other job sites. Something different had happened in that work environment that pulled the subcontractors and vendors working for a purpose. Richard Robichaud had understood the power of that secret years ago as he developed his business. Even in his old age, with arthritis and age spots, he still had that wisdom. Drew wanted that it that people talk about that magic. What was that missing piece? The missing piece still eluded him. It wasn't in his football play. He knew it. That's why he still sat on the bench. The team virtually ignored him, and he had no impact on its success. Drew felt the frustration that he frequently had to smother and drive back down to the pit of his stomach. He had been a star player in college and high school. He was the one to lead the team. Now he only led the way to the team bus as the players scrambled from another city after another dismal game in front of the other team's fans with a documented blunder captured by a camera operator streaming the embarrassing moment to the network and cable outlets. Drew believed his family turned their heads ninety degrees away and pushed the volume down on the television when they saw my jersey driven to the ground again. *These will be my memories of my career in my golden years,* Drew thought to himself. He finally slowed to a walk as he approached the driveway. A flash came to his mind of the Farmers. They were all exasperatingly pleasant to be around. Darla's mother still hadn't given up on that painting on the wall. Drew thought she was the perfect likeness to a beautiful magnolia on the outside, but her inner determination was as strong as an oversized defensive lineman. What is her price? Drew had to wonder. Then there's Danny. Drew liked Danny even when he drove slower than Drew's Papaw Robichaud. Drew concluded that it was because Danny wanted to look at everything while driving. Drew had never been around any guy like that in his entire life. Danny didn't just smell the darn roses. He watched the stars, felt the breeze on his face before making a putt, and smelled rain coming from miles away, even when the sky was blue. He was more accurate than the local meteorologist. When Danny was on the old route to Brunswick, Drew put his foot down one day. That blonde fur bear impersonating a lifeguard from San Diego with his glowing tan insisted on stopping at more than one fruit stand on the way to a golf game. Drew smiled to himself. He warned anyone who did not agree to stop at Danny's request. Danny had a way of hinting at a poker game or making a bet with a nice little pot. He never lost; that's all Drew could say. From his own experience, Drew knew that it was to one's benefit to read the signs that said fresh strawberries next right.

Drew had to shake his head and know that it takes different folks in this world, and at least Danny was the kind that made you smile during the ride. He stopped for a moment before walking up the stairs of the garage to the loft. He looked around and saw the camellias still in bloom, something he would normally not even notice. Danny's sister was like a painting that conjured up desires and admiral qualities of a more tender sort. He found a sense of protectiveness in himself that was an unfamiliar experience. It was a forgotten or ignored emotion along the way. Drew suspected he had that trait earlier in his life. Drew remembered running faster than some of the wide receivers in the league the day Phoebe was planting flowers in Jesse's backyard and screamed when she saw a snake slithering from the bag of dirt she was using.

"That snake never knew what slung his reptile carcass to Omaha!" Jesse joked as he elaborated on the story with others during a cookout the next day.

Drew agreed that was the quickest release with the most extended depth he had ever thrown an object with skin, even with the aid of a shovel. He boasted that working on that throwing arm with the new trainer had done some good in the off-season.

Yes, he thought to himself with a sense of sadness. *I wish I could bottle them up and take them back with me during the season*. It was true he would be leaving soon for the athletic compound near the lake in Northeast Georgia and his home nearby. Searching the cottage had been inspiring this off-season. He found a treasure last night when he found a box of Charley's things that Ali had stored in a closet in the loft marked Charley's sermons. It suggested that she knew Drew would someday return to the cottage and find the little chests of surprises she had kept over the years. The marked box with sermonslabled on it had a simple note inside.

I listened to every line of this sermon and can tell you this is the most boring sermon I have ever heard from anyone living or dead. It took me two scotch on the rocks to listen to the entire cassette, which I faithfully did. With reflection, I can earnestly say, I would rather listen to your dry ramblings bestowing the virtues of this one begetting that one and was the father to this one than any other sermon knowing that you walked the walk and heard the burning bush too. I'm honored to be your friend. Frogman

Drew reasoned that someone must know who the person named Frogman who's name was on the note. *For his grandmother to have kept it all this time, it must have meant something dear to both.* Drew wasn't that much into keeping sentimental things, but he felt he wanted to know more about this story? He paused for a moment. *Where had he heard something like that before?*

Chapter 4

THE SUMMER HAD PASSED. Drew returned to the shores and the people he had become to experience as home when he could. The salty air cleared out the old and brought something fresh and healthy. The athletic trainer and offensive coordinator both agreed Drew's throwing arm seemed more robust this year. There was a lot more velocity and distance with the throws. He also had a better feel for the target and timing during the practice runs through the plays. He went through the motions of learning the plays, keeping his workouts productive. Drew Taylor engaged and got to know the inexperienced players on the roster. Future stars were waiting their turn to be discovered during spring training. Fresh faces with eager hearts. *What's not to like?*

What's not to be jealous of knowing it was him just three years ago? He had been the backup quarterback, a team member unnoticed and silent except in emergencies. *That is unless your number one gun is out of commission.* This year he came to spring training with a distinct set of thoughts filtering on those black thoughts of depression from the year before. He was more than football. Drew has spent a great off-season doing something and connecting with things that mattered more than just the game and the team. Spending some time on the coast was satisfying, in a deep sense. Phoebe was part of that difference, and he realized that. It was an odd feeling. He always thought he had a strong family support base. Now the family felt larger.

Growing up, Drew attended schools his parents selected because they met the proper criteria. Football came with a different group of backgrounds. But a small group of coaches and recruiters defined what the player needed to be successful. A laundry list of desired attributes became a formula.

Drew was glad his mind didn't have to wrestle with those mighty decisions. But where did the heart come into the criteria of who became successful in life? Lately, Drew had pondered this idea a lot. He also knew the mental aspect of the game was important. Then, one day at the end of summer, Drew's head received a message during an exhibition game in August. As the huddle broke and before the play was called, the center heard Drew say, "That's how he does it!" He proceeded to spew the numbers for the play with conviction. Drew rushed for twenty-eight yards in that same play before the other team could race fast enough to pull him down. When asked later how he pulled off the play, Drew shrugged his shoulders and spoke. "I've spent a lot of money on strawberries this year."

In game three of the regular season, an event occurred that pulled Drew out into the attention of the football community.

The first-string quarter-back went out for the rest of the year with an injury in the third quarter. Drew's team was losing at the time, 17-3. Drew filled the slot, jogging out to the huddle. The center looked straight into Drew's eyes and asked, "How much were those strawberries?" Drew looked back at him with the same spirit of grit and yelled to the group. "Enough to make them rue the day they messed with Drew and his brothers!" They won that game 21-17. After that game, a bottle of strawberry wine appeared in a special gift box at his locker. One day one of the rookies made the mistake of teasing Drew about his choice of liquor. That rookie never repeated a word after a wide-shouldered lineman walked in front of the rookie.

"What did you just say?" Cid asked, coming to protect him like a brown bear guards her cubs against a predator.

Drew finished dressing and went over to the young man after he got dressed. "You'll figure it out someday. How about coming over Friday and playing poker? Cid likes to eat barbeque more than tight ends," and patted the rookie on the shoulders with a gentle smile. "We are just family here."

For several weeks in a row, the points on Drew's team were larger than those of the opposing team. With more success, more people noticed him. Drew had the urge for the first time to share their attention with someone other than his teammates. More invites were coming in, and more people wanted to move into his sphere. Phoebe brought along her parents during a home game. Her parents had rented a home in his same gated community for a long weekend. Danny, his wife, and Uncle

Jesse had arrived separately and had a tailgate party at the rental with a lovely couple who lived next door. He never felt so nursed back to health with his bruises and pains. He stretched out his limbs on the lounger. Phoebe drew up a flannel coverlet, wrapping it around them both. The screened porch, with a mix of people, pets, and wildlife, engaged with each other as if it was a reunion. An owl watched from a branch of a tree where the tree line began. A doe walked near the opening and across the lawn to the next property. When Drew quietly asked Phoebe to come to his home, she agreed. His brief time alone with her before returning to the coast thrilled him.

"It's a guy's cave," Phoebe teased when she entered the home from around the first-floor door where Drew was standing. Filling most of the space on one end of the room was a large pool table. A game table with soft overstuffed leather chairs looked ready for a Friday night game. Someone made a large table into a desk and positioned it so he could look out at the expanse of the wooded scene beyond the glass.

Phoebe experienced the sensations of smelling musk and rich spices with the dark rich colors of the forest engulfing her in fabric and artwork on display. No modern chrome or shades of powdery gray on this spot on the hill. It was power and patina, rich and masculine, in one room. "This is nice," she said as she came in and looked around the room with Drew's guidance. "It doesn't feel like my whirling wind vane picking up the light sea breeze." She touched the arm of a leather chair with faux fur and a striped animal pillow and smiled back at Drew with a twinkle in her eye.

Drew had learned that was her way of luring him into her feminine wiles, and he didn't mind. Drew smiled at her playful banter and responded, "No, it doesn't. The décor is a little different upstairs.

You might say we entered the den; you know where we guys go when we have stinky sweat clothes, leave out belches, and talk like sailors."

Phoebe looked at his face intently. "I don't see you as a belcher," she teased. She walked gracefully to the window touching the desk and then the window that took up most of the wall. "I can see you sitting here in deep thought." Phoebe imagined the green foliage and the mountain peaks that one could see in the daylight. A haze would drape the distant highlands. Then her mind pictured another scene. "I can see you holding a strong cup of coffee in the winter, watching the snowflakes outside the window."

"Why do you say that?"

"Because you are strong and disciplined, your coffee would reflect those virtues." She looked back at him. "But you also value natural beauty so you wouldn't be able to resist the charms of the snowflakes as they swirl and fall, making a glistening white blanket outside. You might even see one of those benevolent fairies, the old ones used to speak of in tales of the mountains." Phoebe walked back to where Drew was standing.

"So, your ghost tales go beyond pirates and candles burning from old mansions along the city streets of Savannah?" Drew asked, and touched Phoebe's jawline.

She reached up to touch his hand and smiled back. "I tell my stories for people to enjoy, but the truth behind them I do not promise. I can only say that I cannot disprove them either, as I was not there. I have things I believe, but they are not the tales I share for entertainment. I am quite clear on the difference!" Phoebe took half a step closer. She pushed herself on tiptoes and whispered in his ear. "Those things come from my heart and have a genuine experience, like the dance of the snowflakes." She lowered herself back down again on flat feet.

Drew cleared his throat and blushed for a second before breaking the silence. "Wow!" Drew paused for a moment to bring himself back to the present. "Let's go upstairs. Wow! I'm disappointed that we expect mid-sixties temperatures tonight. Too bad, as I would have wished for a snow squall tonight after your description. However, I won't be able to see another snowfall quite the same after hearing your description." He smiled as he took Phoebe by the hand and started up the stairs.

The upstairs was a different décor than the level on the first floor. Drew had a designer to select the right furnishings and art pieces to provide a feeling of elegance with a masculine twist.

"So, this is where you hang out when you're taking my calls. I can visualize you folding your undies and matching your socks right here as Phoebe moved to the center of the room, touching the soft leather of the L-shaped sofa perpendicular to the window to face the fieldstone fireplace. Phoebe laughed with sheer mischief in her eyes. “Yes, there would be a suitable spot to put the phone on speaker and let me go about my day while you stretch your muscles on this sofa. How could you even listen to my simple tales when this is your castle? Drew, you are here in this rustic palace while I clean oyster shells on a table covered with Sunday’s newspaper. I’m on the porch with my hair tumbling in complete disarray and can’t put the loose strands under my baseball cap because of my slimy hands. Pelican’s eye me with a predator’s intent a few feet away while you comfortably lounge

in comfort.”

“When you say it like that, I wonder who has it better in life. Have I not always been attentive to our conversations?” Drew responded flatly.

“Yes, you speak to me as if I am with you wherever you are. Sometimes the locker room chats are most interesting!” Phoebe laughed, squeezing Drew’s hand.

“I agree with that. But I have grown fond of the differences. I am glad you and your family came here this weekend. I’ve wanted to share a little of what it’s like being around me on this crazy side of the world.

Phoebe stood quietly for a moment. Then ventured on into more conversation. “Did you plan this all yourself?” Phoebe asked.

“Yes, and no. I had an idea. I shared it with Grandfather and Steven. They gave me some suggestions, and I found someone I could work with to help me customize the plans. The contract finished the cabin after my first year as a pro player. I haven't changed it much. I'm rarely here. I wanted to feel the space out first before I made suggestions."

"That's a smart idea. Movement is important. I love this grand entrance. This level is more elegant. It shows off your classical tastes and personality." Phoebe said as she touched his hand again to lead him toward the opening into the large room.

Drew watched her expression as she looked ahead and then looked back as a child would, looking for affirmation that this was the right path. When she reached the next room, her face lit up like a child, as if she spotted a new bike or puppy. He loved to see her joy and the radiance of her expression not dulled by the low lights of the room.

"May I?" she asked with a big smile. After an affirming nod from Drew, she walked to the piano at the far end of the room. She played some popular melodies that were familiar to Drew. She gazed over at him, luring his attention and unconsciously seeking his affection. Phoebe was succeeding at both. After a few minutes, her face took on a more serious expression. She began a classical piece.

Drew remembered the melody from his past when he took Music Appreciation 107 for four credits in college. He was required to watch a dress rehearsal of a ballet performance at the theater for four credits. It was a blessing, given he needed to rest his shoulder after the morning workouts.

Phoebe stopped. She looked up at Drew's eyes like a doe and made a request. "Would you play something for me?"

Drew looked at her and sat down on the piano bench without saying a word. He took a few seconds to stretch out his fingers over the keys. Finally, he responded, "Few people know I can play. Don't tell the guys. I may be the next Christmas party entertainment the way players' salaries keep rising. Besides, they'll need me for something when Bowman comes off the disabled list next year."

Phoebe touched his sore arm with a gentle massage and worked up his shoulders. Her hands worked in rhythm to the music. After a few minutes, she walked over to the side of the instrument, stretching her form along its line. She made one twirl and then put both hands back on the piano's surface, closing her eyes and listening to the notes. When Drew finished, she looked at him with glassy but sparkling eyes. He saw her lipstick, red, like the French women who don't wear layers of makeup to express feminine beauty. Phoebe expressed that gift in front of his eyes.

"I see a beautiful ballerina," Drew remarked as he stopped pressing on the keys.

"Uncle Jesse calls me a mermaid," Phoebe said, breaking up the moment's intensity.

"That's perfectly acceptable for him as your uncle. I am not your good uncle

or your twin brother."

"That's true, but we have become friends, haven't we?"

"I think you know this is moving past that point."

Phoebe smiled back. "I like that. I just need time."

"Phoebe, I'm not patient. You already have me twisted up like a pretzel. That gives me the fuel to play like I've been playing. I need an answer from you."

Phoebe avoided giving Drew a direct answer. Instead, diverting his attention by gently pulling his hand out to the balcony, she could dodge responding to a commitment she wasn't ready to make yet. Finally, after another hour of dodging and deflecting a direct answer, Phoebe stated she needed to get back. "It's getting late, and I need to return to my parent's rental." She looked at Drew with doe-like eyes as she sat in her car, ready to leave. "I will send you an answer soon."

Drew remembered hearing Phoebe's words before she left his home last night. He watched her headlights snake down the darkened lane from his home to the rental the Farmers were staying at tonight. They planned to leave tomorrow, and he already felt the loss.

Several weeks passed by since Drew had seen Phoebe. The holidays would soon be coming. He made plans, and then there were games. He had to reach specific deadlines. Yet he most wanted to fly to Savannah and watch that red and teal wind vane twirl until sunset. He wanted to feel the soft blanket tickling his neck, and the perfectly shaped, sparking violet eyes peeping up at him. His beautiful ballet dancer with her golden streaked hair just reaching above the covering with her torso curled next to his brawny, bruised, and scarred frame. Listening to the Atlantic Ocean crashing against the Northern continent was all he wanted for Christmas this year. He groaned to himself. *I feel parched and in need of water in the desert.*

When he sat on the bench for two years in a row and went home with another loss in his belt without taking a handoff from the center, all he wanted to do was play football. Now he is the man in the limelight and would rather have another piece of the pie. News reporters wanted to talk with him. Magazines want his smiling, fresh face for their covers. Drew took it all in stride, but he wished Phoebe was a part of this portion of his life. The weeks were counting down closer to Thanksgiving. The team played their hearts out during the Thursday night game against a solid Texas team. Stepping away with a win in overtime was a real punch in Drew's confidence. Drew wished he could have had more time to talk to a couple of college teammates, but he was being shuffled off the field and into the locker room before he could congratulate the kicker who made the last field goal. Drew kept his comments gracious but brief, trying to find his way to his locker. There it was on the bench like every other home game since he started playing for the injured first-string quarterback. He looked around and saw the player he suspected had arranged for the box, the team's center, all six feet of him. "You know Jordan; strawberry wine seems

to be somebody's favorite."

Cid blankly looked at Drew and said, "It's not from me, Drew. It seems like Santa Claus has his eye on the game. So, they must have the game playing in the elf shop."

"Your hopeless, Cid. All I know is if there's ever a contract to trade you, they better put my name in the loopholes. I'm not standing behind anyone else but you in a game. I know who's protecting my nose and limbs out there."

"I would like to take credit, my friend, but it's not me who's got you covered."

"What do you mean by that?"

Cid shook his head and responded. "It's not me that's calling out the signals. That's your role."

"It's part of the game, and those are the calls I'm getting from the sidelines."

"You believe that? I've seen the drills. Those calls didn't come from the sideline, at least not initially. Like, where did they come from, man? Did we steal a rule book?"

"What? I'm calling them as I hear them!" Drew stated in frustration, blind to his teammate's meaning.

"Listen, my friend. Something is filling you with those calls, and I know that means my job is to protect you. So, you follow your purpose." Cid said quietly and put his hand on Drew's shoulder.

Just then, a reporter came to interview Drew about the game. The moment was gone in the frenzy of the media and antics of the locker room sideshow. *What was Cid implying anyhow?*

A couple more weeks passed. It was after the final game before Thanksgiving, and Drew was lamenting to himself on paper on the flight coming back from a game in Texas. He had scribbled on paper. *My thoughts betray me. The game is over. My cravings for a specific sugar-stuffed temptation found near a coastal causeway due east is taking over my life.* Drew continued to wrestle with his thoughts. She hadn't said yes yet. Finally, Thanksgiving was just a few days away. Phoebe promised me she would give me an answer by Thanksgiving. For two weeks, Drew received no word regarding her decision. Phoebe had asked for time, but enough of her postponements. Drew crossed out his confession before the plane arrived. Letting these rascals know what he was thinking was not a smart idea. As for the object of his obsession, he could only hope that what he wanted was there the next time he pulled into the lot of the sweet little shop near the watery marsh. Better yet, it needed to be packed and ready to go when he arrived.

Twenty minutes before landing, the team's offensive line coordinator, Sam Barnes, walked up through the aisle.

"I thought I would let Bussey stretch out over two seats, and I saw a seat up here open. I hope you don't mind."

"Not at all, Sam." Drew asked about some things on his mind. "Sam, am I screwing up with the plays?"

"Why do you ask that?"

Drew took a deep breath. "I just play the game. I learn plays each week and try to learn the defensive line with each competitor. I'm not sure if I'm in the right mindset."

"You're making points, aren't you? Everybody seems to go where you called them to be. Nobody is getting hurt. That was not the case with the referee last week, but he wasn't in the place he was supposed to be when the play was in action. I can't regret him getting a shiner. I never liked that pompous referee, anyway. Last year when he made that... I digress. It was an accident, though. Drew, I was part of the group that wanted you on our team when we picked you during the college draft. We saw a guy who could throw a bullet, and his movements were sleek like a panther. I know it must have taken some steam out of your sail to sit on the bench for the last three years. I'm glad you're getting your day in the lights."

"Thanks, Sam. I appreciate that. So, who do I need to thank for the strawberry wine that keeps showing up at my locker? You know everything that goes on in that locker room. So, who do I need to thank?"

"It's not that big of a deal. I bring it, and I get one of the athletic trainers to put it next to your locker at each home game before the buzzer at the end of the fourth quarter goes off."

"Wait! It's you who brings the wine?" Drew's expression became animated as his eyes staring at Sam with black saucers and mouth wide open. Drew was left speechless.

"Yes, I heard you comment on the offensive line about the story of strawberries and something to do with a poker match. I didn't hear the whole thing. I play golf sometimes when I'm over on the coast with some friends. One guy said that he knew you and that you had a special fondness for the stuff. He is a part owner of a wine-making company that makes strawberry wine. My understanding is that it is an elite private label. The wine's a custom blend and not produced in massive quantities. I'm not much of a wine person, but my wife likes it a lot, especially in summer as a summer cooler. He's been sending me a bottle for you every home game. He said to keep it anonymous. This last package was a little different. He said that if you should ask, tell Drew, 'She packed the box herself.' Those are the words he told me to say. I assumed you knew the female in question?" Sam looked at Drew with a questioning face.

"Oh, Sam, I love you. I could kiss you on the lips right now, but I'm going to hold back the urge. I have a plan now to save myself for someone a lot prettier! I opened none of the boxes after the first one. I just took them home and stored them away. I bet Phoebe has given me an answer already! I didn't even open the boxes. I guess I didn't want the ribbing over strawberry wine. I thought it was a guy teasing me about something I said once about the playing the entire game. Big Cid defended me one day from one of the inexperienced players who thought to tease me. I let all the other boxes untouched. Shoot, I want to get my hands on those boxes! I gave her a promise. I would never be embarrassed by anything about her. I stepped into the trap this time, didn't I?"

"I can't wait to hear the story on this one!" Sam said with a laugh. "She must be a diamond that you have been hiding. I speculate that this dove of yours has a sun-kissed complexion, natural blond tresses, and wears a spaghetti string sun dress and sandals when you ride around on the coast in that convertible of yours. She smells like a bouquet of spring flowers. Every time she moves closer to turn the radio station, you take in another whiff of her fragrance, causing you to remember her long after you've taken her home."

"Well said, my friend. I didn't know you were so poetic about the female species. You don't talk to us like that on the field."

Sam shrugged his shoulders. "Why would I use my best lines on the guys?

Besides, I was single once too."

After a few moments, Sam got more serious, and his voice dropped in volume. "Do you think there's anything she is uncomfortable with you knowing, Drew? Most girls dating the star quarterback called her best friends, her hairdresser, her first-grade teacher, and every magazine editor around. I am betting she is beautiful and glows like a burning bush when she is out in the sunshine and brings light when she sits in the darkness of night."

Surprise took Drew by the description. "I only know of a burning bush that calls out people in the Bible. I can't remember exactly where."

"That's a starting point, I guess/" Same took the discussion in another direction. "I know you, Drew. I would bet in Vegas that she is a beautiful woman. I know your tastes. I also know that women gifted in beauty tend to enjoy the attention of being linked with someone in the spotlight. It's their gift to the world. She's keeping herself from shining, from what I can infer. It could mean she's a keeper and wants to respect your privacy like hers. However, I'm sensing she has a reason she wants to be private, which is holding her back from shining on her favorite man's arm. You've met her family and where she lives, so that's not the unknown. She's been here and lets you spend time with her in open places, right?"

"Yes, to all." Drew was trying to follow Sam's line of thought.

"Do you think she's dated anyone on the team or in the circus following the team?"

"No, not that she has told me about, anyway. I don't know. She lived in New England for a few years during college and for a brief time after graduation. She doesn't hint about knowing a lot about football past casual knowledge. You know she doesn't talk about the time after college much. She talks about dance, some of her college experiences, and the sea. The southern coast is in her blood. That is what she freely speaks about the most. She talks about fashion, the bakery, the arts, music, books, current events, and things like deep-water fishing and sea creatures. Loggerhead turtles are something she loved to talk about. That was one of her grandfather's favorite research topics before he retired. She is so interesting to listen to and funny. Her name is Phoebe, and she is a twin. Phoebe is so tender-hearted and cares for animals. You have me thinking, Sam. There are a lot of things I don't know about her."

"That's a truth that will last a whole lifetime. You think you know your wife? Then, one day, she hits you with a shocking surprise. For example, my wife told me this week that we may need to redecorate my older son's room and put him with his younger brother. I thought she was crazy. I told her in not-such-pleasant words that there was no chance junior would fall for that suggestion. Then, she says we have about six months to warm him up to the idea. I look at her, and she smiles. I bellowed some words I will edit for this conversation. That started Abbie crying. Talk about making an utter fool of myself and needing to eat my words with humble cod liver oil to make it go down easier. But I am happy about it. I am!"

"Congratulations, Sam. I can't think of a better father for your kids or a better parent at all those teacher-parent conferences in your future."

"If my three boys are like me. I'm sure I will have the school on speed dial and know the principal's secretary on a first-name basis by the end of the first four weeks. The first week will be the honeymoon period for all of them. Thank goodness my wife is great with people."

"I appreciate your wisdom, Sam. You have me thinking about a lot of things. You are more than an OC," Drew responded with a grin.

"I know that. However, the offensive line in front of you needs reminders occasionally."

"Branson, are you awake up there?" Sam touched the left shoulder of the man in the seat in front of him, pointing to the seat belt light showing overhead. "It's time to wake up!" Sam yelled out. He patted Drew's shoulder and got up to move back to his original seat.

The aircraft became animated, and the landing gear dropped for the aircraft's final descent. Thoughts of returning home after the game in Pennsylvania felt a bit more distant as he walked down the steps to the waiting bus. The home was where he wanted to be. When Drew finally arrived at his mountainside residence, he attempted to call Phoebe, but no answer. Eventually, he left a vague greeting on her voicemail and promised to try back tomorrow. Another game had passed with a win added to the team's total for the year. Drew had never been this close to the division playoffs in three years, and neither had most of the team members. He called his mother's number but was an hour behind his time zone.

"Your grandparents were here with us watching the entire game," CeCe said. "We had a house full of people. Of course, I had to take the cell phone away from your grandfather. The grandchildren showed him how to create and use one of the social media accounts. We thought it was best to eliminate any risk during the game. I want the family to be allowed to attend the Christmas service this year in our parish. You know how colorful he can be. I was glad I did after watching the play when your coach sent in a rushing play at the end of the third quarter. I'm sure you remember the one I'm talking about with those other team shirts covering you behind the line of scrimmage. I had to put your grandfather in the penalty box for non-sportsmen-like language and make him let out the dogs just to cool him down."

Drew had to laugh at the image. Grandfather Robichaud was 80 years old, still humorous and fiery, with a soft heart. Yet, he never lost that spirit. Richard had made his reputation as a trailblazer in the commercial building industry, using environmentally safer materials than the day's standard. He was a tornadic force to deal with in his younger years, but he more than not attempted to do the right thing. His family adored him with all his speckles, freckles, and warts.

"Mother, I don't know my plans for Christmas yet, but I'm thinking of being in Savannah. If I was there, would you and Kyle like to celebrate Christmas there even if it wasn't on Christmas day?"

"That's a thought, son. Is there a particular reason?"

"Yes, and no. I want to check on the house and spend some time with Phoebe and her family. I'm starting to feel like they're family too. But I also know it's our family tradition to be together. We play in Florida the week before Christmas and then a home game the week after. I think Christmas Eve might be an enjoyable way of having the family together somewhere, even if we celebrate in the middle of the week. I say I would like to be in Savannah, but if the schedule is such that I must be here, we could all meet here. We had a fun time when Phoebe's family rented a house just down the street for a long

weekend."

"Drew, if that's what you want, we will go wherever you want to spend the holiday together. I can answer this for Kyle as well. It sounds to me like you are planning something, Drew. Would you like to tell me anything more?"

"No, not really. I'm always thinking of football, right?"

CeCe responded, "No, Drew, football is never to be the first in your heart. I have taught you that since you were young. I think you don't want to say more so that you won't lie to your mother, so I won't force you to tell me anything. We will be happy to know more about your plans when you have decided."

"Thank you, Mother," Drew said without elaborating. He ended the call on a light note and turned his thoughts to something else that entered his mind.

Several public socials were coming up in Drew's life that he would be obligated to attend. He had, on several occasions, asked Phoebe if she wanted to attend as his date. She always declined. That concerned him more. Drew could not figure out the refusal. He was sure her feelings were mutual. He couldn't spend much time during the season with her, which was hard on most couples who shared the life of the circus, one city one week and another the next. Many females were flocking in his direction, but the one he wanted the most was the hardest to catch. One shouldn't try to capture the sunlight, he thought. Drew didn't know more about how he could get her to commit to him and his life. Yet he saw her glow like a diamond. She danced at the side of the piano in his home in the mountains like a burning bush. Her violet eyes flickered from the candlelight, sending him a message. Watch me dance. Then she stopped her pirouette. He now thought of the story about Moses and wondered what it all meant. What does that have to do with me? Drew remembered the night so many times when he was alone. The vision replayed in his mind. Sam asked if there was something she was uncomfortable with, which is why she preferred to stay hidden. Drew didn't want to follow that path of thought. Moving her away from her family was a big concern. Drew wasn't sure if he could remove that obstacle. He was willing to look at alternatives if she was willing to be more open to some lifestyle changes. Then there were the boxes awaiting him. He knew he had to look at them closer. Drew poured himself some hot coffee and went downstairs to look further at the eight rose and gold boxes he had stored away. How could he tell which one was hers? He picked up the first. There was no distribution label on the box, only an embossed message across the top of the lid saying Secret Label. Pulling out the bottle, he could see the sticker made for the bottle with an image of a strawberry on a vine, the logo for the distributing company circling the sticker. Nothing mysterious about the label. He looked at the packaging again. He then noticed a black ribbon that looped in the lid of the box. Drew wondered at that and pulled the tab to remove the covering.

It said, *congratulations*. Drew thought this was better, but not it. So next, he opened a second box with a similar graphic. This time it had Drew's shirt number. There was writing on the label.

Best game ever!

Drew laughed because this bottle had the date received. It was his best game ever. He finally came to the two remaining boxes, and he knew from seeing where he had opened them that that box was the first, so he passed over it and went to the remaining box. Drew touched the bottle for a few minutes savoring the idea that Phoebe had embraced the same box. Then, he gently opened the box, saw the same bottle, and looked at the lid. Then, he pulled on the loop. This time there was an illustration of him sitting on the bench just like in the photo that was in the paper. Still, this illustration added his of a female player with long blond hair pulled back in a ponytail like the first time he saw her at the bakery—*a lifetime with you, P.F.*

By now, it was 1:00 in the morning. Drew decided he wouldn't wake Phoebe in the middle of the night. He walked out to the patio and looked up at the indigo sky. He found the most brilliant star and texted a message to her. A star sent to protect and cherish until I can reach you.

Across the state, Phoebe sat by her bedroom window, looking over the sand into the silvery ribbons of the incoming tide with a full moon reflecting light from above. She heard the vibration on her phone. Phoebe walked across the room to her phone on the vanity. She read the text on her phone and carried it to the front of the mirror. Phoebe raised her night dress and moved her left leg in an extension once performed with elegance. She broke down in tears and moved back to the window she had been sitting at, watching the silvery waves. In Phoebe's heart, she sobbed, God, are you awake? Drew spent two more days with the team before heading east. He wouldn't get in until late Tuesday night. Wednesday would be satisfactory to complete the most important things on his list.

Upon arrival, he saw a porch light at Jesse Farmer's home. Drew took out the keys for the garage and loft and bound up the stairs to put his things down. He looked around briefly and found everything as it should be. He brought some simple supplies with him so he wouldn't have to find something open late at night. There was nothing wrong with a peanut butter and jelly sandwich in a pinch when one could eat it under the stars in Drew's favorite spot in the studio over the garage. He could sleep in, take a run, and then stop in the bakery between the breakfast and the lunch crowd. Drew received a text from Jesse a little after he had the lights on in the loft. Phoebe's uncle invited him to come over and socialize. He wanted to refuse, but it was just next door since it was Phoebe's uncle. He would walk over and at least say hello before calling it a night.

Jesse called him in the front door as soon as Drew crossed the property lines. Good to see you back, Drew. I won't keep you up late, but since I had somebody here, you should meet. I thought this might be an excellent chance to get you both in the same place at the same time.

Drew walked in the front door and back to the family room at the back of the house. He could hear something like music from the room beyond. However, he wasn't sure it had a melody.

"Drew, let me introduce you to Ian McLoughlin. He's a friend and somewhat of a business partner of mine."

Drew looked a little surprised for a moment. So, this is the competition, Drew thought. How convenient it was to run into the only guy he was aware of who posed a threat to steal Phoebe away from him. Drew was wary of the situation he was walking into, but he exchanged the typical handshakes and social greetings.

Jesse poured a pint of beer and put it down in front of the chair he had directed Drew to take. We've been hanging out here tonight, trying out some tentative melodies Ian has put together while he was on the road. I did some music work when I was younger. I met Ian and the band when they started the business. They kept going, and I grew tired of the stuff that goes with making music other than playing on a stage. I wasn't met for the big show and bus rides. We've stayed friends over the years.

Ian, trying to keep the conversation, chimed in. "So, how does it feel to be this close to the playoffs? I haven't been able to watch all the games, but I have caught a few. I will admit soccer is more to my understanding, but anything with a leather ball is fun to me."

Drew smiled, easing up a bit. "It's more fun when you win on the plane ride home. I can say that. I can also say I'm getting more of a physical workout this year than my year on the bend."

"Yeah, I bet that is the truth!" Ian responded. "Do you think the chances are good for the team to go the entire way this year?"

"I think we have as good of a chance as any other team. I'm just one player. I'm not out there alone getting things done. The rest have their mission, too.?"

"That sounds very diplomatic, Drew. So, are you set up next door? Do you need anything?"

"No, the place is ready for me when I come into town. I just show up."

"I have some jambalaya on the stove. Would you like some now?" Jesse asked. "I'm going to put some in a container to take over with you."

"You know that sounds good, but I think I will take it as a to-go box if you don't mind. I have a lot to do tomorrow so I won't be up to late." Two hours later, Drew was about ready to call it a night. He could play Ian's acoustic guitar while the musician hammered out a tune on his 12-string guitar. Jesse chimed in with his base. The rockers were not a threat to the crowd on the charts, but it was an enjoyable evening different from Drew's typical evening that ranged from poker chips with the guys to black tie affairs with champagne. Jesse occupied himself in another room for a few minutes, so Drew asked Ian some questions on his mind since he walked into the room tonight and met the code word Rock Muffin in person. Drew knew Ian had known Phoebe outside the bakery. Drew faced Ian with cold steel eyes. "Why does Phoebe choose to work in the bakery and not dance?"

"She has her reasons for not being in the public view, right or wrong," Ian responded. "She works with many of the injured sea turtles, especially the ones that a propeller from boats has hurt. So, she feels connected to them."

Drew asked, "Did you ever take her out for dinner or go on a date?"

"No," Ian responded. "She deserves someone greater, more refined than my circle of bad boys and me. No one can appreciate a diamond's beauty in the wrong element. It needs to shine. She's a diamond meant for a crown for someone who can experience her elegance and beauty. I have a little crush on that little dove, and I would break the arm of anyone who would break her heart or harm her again. I think we understand each other. The Farmers and I have a platonic and business relationship. That is all." It was a deliberate attempt by Ian to move to a more neutral turf. He raised his hand with the dark frothy lager.

Jesse returned to the room with a small pot of his Cajun Creole cuisine and put it in Drew's arms. My gumbo will give you some heat if the chilly breeze keeps blowing inland.

"Thanks, man," Drew responded and started walking to the door. Before turning the knob. Drew looked back and saw a bottle of strawberry wine on the liquor cabinet." Drew took a moment and said, "Hey, thanks for the wine. It was a nice touch after every game." Jesse looked puzzled for a minute.

"The gift wasn't from me, Drew."

When Ian stood in the hallway with his packed-up gear, Drew was ready to say something more. Instead, however, Ian interjected into the conversation. "I sent it, Drew. Phoebe can tell you more tomorrow. Sam and I have been friends for the last four years. I had this idea, and Sam agreed to work with me. I wanted to celebrate this tremendous accomplishment. You kept winning, so it was more than a fluke. Someone got this fire started in the locker room."

Drew walked back and hugged Ian. "I don't know what has happened in the last twelve months, but something has taken hold of my world and has given it a good shake-up. I appreciate your interest. I do!" Drew walked to the door again and looked over at Jesse. "You're from a crazy world, Jesse Farmer, but I'm starting to love every moment I'm in it." Drew walked out and back to the property next door.

Chapter 5

THE THANKSGIVING HOLIDAY WAS the real thing at the Farmer's household. It started on the Tuesday before Thanksgiving as a part of the Fall Festival at a church. The location was not the church the Farmers attended. Instead, this was where they went to remember Charley and now Ali. The tradition continued with help from several vital businesses and citizens in the area. By 5:00 in the morning, the action had begun. Inside the church kitchen, an assembly line put order to the chaos of supplies. As the morning progressed, a group of strangers worked together to pull off breakfast for those who came to receive a hot meal. Some volunteers gathered boxes for those someone who cared had added whose names to a list. Those packages would be hand-delivered.

Darla and her husband took care of the donations that came through the back door from the parking lot. Their eyebrows raised when Drew and a driver came in with a rental truck around 8:30 AM, filled with additional donations from a donut chain. The company's owner lived across the state line in South

Carolina and was Drew's friend. Danny and his wife assumed coffee operations. Others filled the gaps in jobs wherever needed.

Drew left the driver once everything was off the truck to find Phoebe. After looking for her and asking around, he saw her across the street. Volunteers were working with the children, decorating the park with an assortment of scarecrows of various themes. "I'm glad I found you," Drew said, putting his hands on her shoulders. "You've been busy."

"Yes, but it's been all fun, right gang!" Phoebe yelled out to the children and volunteers standing around her.

Voices cheered back, "Yeah!"

"Drew, I want you to meet Kenya. He wants to become a football player, and I've not been much help.

"Well, Kenya, I might help you out. I play a little football.I got an idea."

Kenya looked up at Drew with weariness.

Drew reached into his back pocket and pulled out one of the team's caps. "I bet putting this on will help you picture a football in your mind, so let's start with that idea." The little boy gladly put the cap on and posed as if he was on the front line in a game.

"I'm sure I've seen a guard in front of me look like that. Now we need something else." Drew took one of the prepared straw dolls donated by one of the local clubs. Kenya grabbed a paintbrush and a little egg carton with some paint. "Now we're talking." Drew showed him where the white lines should go to make the numbers on the doll's shirt. And Kenya used white paint to make the white lines for the number 11. Drew then directed Kenya to pick a plastic football that was part of some of the donated art supplies. The box also had a plastic helmet that would fit perfectly over the straw. Kenya could finish the player except for one other touch.

"Phoebe, I know you have the drawing skills to finish this perfectly. Could you add a mascot right here in the center of the helmet?"

Drew looked over at Kenya. "What should the mascot be?"

Kenya answered back, "A cheetah!" Phoebe responded. "A cheetah it is! Kenya, you gave me a challenge with that one, but I think I can draw something that will work." She took the marker offered by Drew and began her sketch. "How is that for a ferocious team mascot?" Kenya gave a big smile.

"Wow!" Kenya responded.

"Now for the best part," Drew said to the little boy and his mother. "We are going to ask if the people distributing the scarecrows around the square will put them in a cool place like an ice cream shop or even a bakery with donuts and cookies. How does that sound?"

Kenya gave a big "yes!"

"Hey, I have a better idea. I bet that firefighters over there would like to take your fall mascot and put it on the firetruck or the fire station. How cool would that be?"

Kenya nodded his head with a big grin.

Drew knelt to put the cheetah in his arm and took Kenya by the hand. After delivering the decoration, the firefighter, Kenya, and his mother walked to the fire truck, where Kenya could proudly place the item in the back seat of the ladder truck. He and his mother then, with a big smile.

Kenya kept looking back at the scarecrow he had made. It proudly rode on the emergency for now. Later, it would go to the station around the corner.

"He didn't know who you were," Phoebe said, and she turned around to look at Drew directly with a smile.

"That's the way I want it to be. I like to be just me with the boys," and he gave Phoebe a wink.

Phoebe opened her mouth in astonishment. "Did Danny tell you to tell me that?"

Drew laughed and kissed her on the forehead. He whispered in her ear. "When does the festival wrap up here?"

Phoebe looked around. "The volunteers started tearing things down and packing up between 10:30 and 11:00 as many of them are busy this time. It's considered a breakfast event, so late risers are a bit out of luck, but it's a fun time for those who get here early." Phoebe wanted to help Drew understand the event's significance to the community. She responded to Drew's interest and explained the morning breakfast is a real treat, especially when the weather has cooled for fall. The timing works out for many volunteers to share Thanksgiving Day with their family and still celebrate a community breakfast on the Tuesday before the holiday. The children in the community get a meal and some fun and that makes their life just a little special."

Drew listened intently. He had never felt real physical hunger, but he appreciated those who had compassion for humanity in this way and supported it with dignity.

"Our family has a tradition of having a late afternoon or early evening family dinner on the Tuesday before Thanksgiving. This year we planned it for the evening. Mother had hoped you would join us, you see. We may not have that big turkey dinner, as the traditional story goes. Sometimes we just have a light meal and go to the beach together, or we'll make a covered dish and pick a house to go to that year. The main thing is that we try to spend some time together for a couple of hours. Food is optional, but it is usually part of the plan."

"I like that," Drew said and moved a golden tress from Phoebe's eye and stared at her. "If you don't mind. I'm going to step away for a few minutes. I might even go into the church and talk to the present pastor if he's there. I'm coming back. When I do, I want you to take me in that vehicle you parked there so you can be alone with me for a few hours."

"Drew, that idea sounds like a dangerous ploy. Are you sure you aren't making a pass?" Phoebe teased.

"No, I'm sure it's not a pass. I have a plan straight from my game book, you see. I am not a guy across a room who is trying to charm a pretty lady for some company for a few hours. That's what my opponent may think, but that's not my intention. You can count on that. I will see you in a few minutes." He held her hand and kissed it before he moved away

After he started walking a few feet away, he turned around. I want to steal you away for a bit. I will get you back in time for tonight. If you're not agreeable to that plan, my Plan B is to call Jerry and request that he return the rental truck, and I kidnap you."

"I like plan A, so off with you, and I will be ready when you return." Phoebe smiled. She loved seeing Drew laugh. She loved seeing him open up and come out of the shell of being on guard with people.

Just then, a youngster asked Drew for his autograph on the back of his hot chocolate cup.

Drew said, "I've got something better. Hold on to that cup, and this lovely lady will help you make an ornament on the tree. It needs a special ornament that only you can make. Now, with this red ornament here, I'm going to sign my name, and I'm going to put your name right here. Jake, this will be your ornament for your tree. How does that sound?"

"Sure!"

"Tell me your name?"

"My name is Michael."

"Drew looked down at this little person and knelt to look him in the eye. "Michael, I want you to have the best Thanksgiving ever!" Drew looked back at Phoebe. "I want Michael to make the best scarecrow of all.

When I come back, I will find your scarecrow, Michael."

Michael grinned and let Phoebe take him to the supplies table to working on a scarecrow .

Drew took a plastic football, signed his name along with his message to Michael, and put it in his hand then looked at Phoebe and said, "I will be back in ten minutes." Drew moved swiftly through the people gathering around and into the church across the street. Inside, the church looked empty upstairs. He sat down in the last pew, made a couple of phone calls, and sat silently for a few minutes. When I was a boy, this was what he remembered worship and prayer were like with his mother. CeCe would light a candle and kneel in the pew. Drew looked around at all the details in the sanctuary. The sanctuary was the space where his grandfather preached his sermons. He suspected there would be singing, as his grandfather loved music. His father had visited this same church when they both were still alive. Now they were in heaven together. Drew wanted to know more about them. What were they like when they were Drew's age? He wanted to hear their voice when they laughed. Drew wanted to see the intimacy of their thoughts. Somehow Phoebe had drawn him there, a place where his father and grandfather had interacted with each other, sharing something like a father and son relationship. He knew they would love Phoebe. She had that same hidden mystery. As he sat for a few more moments alone on the pew, Drew felt a comforting sensation come over him. He could sense the true meaning of a Bible verse his mother had told him many times growing up. He recognized a felt the words on the inside. I won't ever leave you, Michael Andrew Taylor. You will never be lost if you hold my hand. Drew felt the tears reach his hands as they rolled off his jaw and chin.

A man put his hand on Drew's shoulder. "I'm glad you came, Drew."

Startled, Drew quickly put his emotions under control and turned around.

"I am Reverend Townsend. I know you from your pictures on the sports channel. I watch the games after church on Sunday. Does that surprise you?"

Drew shrugged his shoulders. For most of the games we played this year, we needed a miracle to win, so I guess it was good to have someone out there praying."

"Some Volunteers said that you brought in a truckload of donations today. I thank you on behalf of all the organizers who worked hard to make this happen. Can I say the chocolate-filled cream puffs were sinful?" Reverend Townsend responded, trying to make a joke to lift the spirit of their conversation.

"Yes, my trainer would probably say that too, but you must have a little fun on this side of heaven, Father."

"Call me Joe; I'm not Catholic, so father and priest don't fit me either. Reverend is so formal. I like Joe. That's what my friends call me. So, Drew, what brought you into church today?"

"I just came in to get away from the people. I thought I could wait till tonight for something, but I don't think I can wait any longer. The doors were open, and I came in."

"Ahh, I presume you want to be alone with someone?"

Drew nodded sheepishly.

"Phoebe Farmer, I presume."

Drew nodded his head again without looking directly into the eyes of the pastor. He didn't like this nervous feeling he was having. Besides, Drew felt embarrassed talking about his feelings to a stranger.

"Would it be that you're thinking of asking Phoebe the big question this weekend?"

Drew looked puzzled that he would know so much.

"Drew, you are hard to hide this year. Plus, you have deep ties here. You take after Charley and your father. They were special people who had a profound impact on others. I have noticed that Phoebe has similar qualities."

"That's my only hesitation. I have felt that I have been missing something these significant people seemed to have."

"I see. You think you are missing something? Losing a father without knowing him might be like having a big emptiness connecting with God."

"I'm not much into religion, Joe. And I am not the only person who lost their father early in life."

"True. There have been many others." Joe paused before saying anything more. "Most people don't accept what they need. They often fall for what they want. Two different things entirely."

"Does this story involve a fast sailboat and angler? I think my grandfather already told me this one." Drew interjected. "I see.

Those stories taste like dry mush sometimes. Dull-like sermons on who begat whom in the Bible are like that for most people."

Drew looked up, and his face was stoic. "Joe, get to what you want to say. If you know something I don't understand, make it clear like water because I must be too thickheaded to understand."

"You're not alone. Your grandfather believed in God because he felt the pain of making mistakes that led him away from a genuine relationship with Him. He walked the road of religion, and it was empty. I suppose wanted to know God in his own heart and wouldn't let go until he found him. Charley Howard walked the way he did because that was who he was on the inside. Michael's life was shorter, but he made the same choice. I am sure of it. That's what brought him to Savannah. God was calling him so that Michael could experience Him. Charley and Ali were the beacons that brought Michael home to His love."

"Joe, I want to grasp what you're saying. I need to do this for Phoebe and myself. I don't want to lose her if I say yes to something I believe is calling me."

"Drew, letting go of His hand is a sure way of letting her go. She's got her heart anchored. Phoebe trusted when darkness came to her door. She won't let go of His hand. I will pray with you; you can stay if you wish for as long as you need. "

Drew remained for a few more minutes after Joe had left the pew. Then, finally, he exited quietly, finding his way across the street. Drew wasn't sure what had happened. But the strangest feeling overcame him, and he wanted to know Frogman. He hungered for what Frogman loved.

Thirty minutes later, Drew and Phoebe traveled down the old highway to South Carolina past the Shrimp boats that docked on the May River.

"So, what are you up to, Drew? You've had this goofy grin since you returned to get me after you went AWOL for ten minutes. I almost texted Pastor Joe to see if you were with him, But I didn't think you'd be there. You are becoming more interesting by the hour. So where are we going? Can you give me a clue, or do you plan to surprise me?" Phoebe kept smiling and looking again at Drew. She didn't say another word for the next few miles.

Finally, Drew turned on a side road and followed it until it came to a dead-end and a large parking lot. There was a marina beyond parking the car in the lot. Drew opened her door and held Phoebe's hand as they walked past the office and down the pier. "I am looking for a boat called the Catalina II with a pilot named Carl. I bet it is that one right over there." Drew and Phoebe walked to the private yacht anchored to the left., which was more of a yacht. A jovial looking man came forward to meet the couple partway down the pier.

"I am Carl Wilton, the captain of the Mermaid II. You must be Mr. Taylor?"

"Yes," Drew said as he shook the boat captain's hand. "This is Phoebe Farmer. We are happy to spend a few hours out on the water today. The Catalina is quite a vessel."

"I am happy to meet you both. Thank you. This vessel is quite a pleasant diversion from the pickup truck I used to get around when I'm not in the water. I live on the island across the way, but I primarily anchor this vessel at this marina. The Catalina has recently traveled down to Key West and up to Maine. I will show you the interior cabin. Watch your step here. When you're ready, come up to the deck from this door in the cabin. It looks like it will be an enjoyable day to sail. The dolphins should be happy to swim along as there is not as much traffic on the water today. The sound can get quite crowded in the sweltering summer with various kinds of boats and paddle boarders."

"Thank you, Carl. If you don't mind, we're going to enjoy some privacy. Is everything ready?"

"Yes, Mr. Taylor. There is an intercom on the wall in the cabin here. So, all you need to do is press the button for assistance."

Drew led the way to the sitting area, which functioned as the living area on board. The roses were waiting, and the champagne was in an ice bucket. "Tell me, Phoebe, how did your father meet your mother?" Drew d uncorked the bottle and select two of the fluted glasses."

"You're going to tease me, aren't you, with all this going on around me? They met at college."

"Who was more attracted to whom first?" Drew asked as he poured the champagne.

"I don't know. It was mutual. My parents never talked about how they dated. Dad just showed up one day and was part of the family. I know they hiked part of the Appalachian trail together.

They said they had wanted to finish the part not completed on their first attempt, but then Drew and I came along soon after they got married, so that goal got deleted." Phoebe giggled when she felt the tingling of the champagne shoot down her throat.

"How did your father show romance to your mother?"

"Are you joking? You've met my father. Do you think there's a romantic thought in that man's head? Every year since I was sixteen, my dad would ask me what to buy for my mother as a present for her birthday. He would always say that he didn't know what she would like. I strongly advised him that anything with an agitator, dry cycle or a hose suck up anything was not arriving at the house for her birthday. Thanks to me, my father listened, and my mother now has the loveliest collection of amethyst jewelry one could ever desire. You must never tell the story to my mother, as I will deny every bit of the truth!"

Drew looked down at her in amusement. "I will have to remember that one. My grandfather gave gifts with leather seats and four tires."

"Now that's fine!" Phoebe teased back. "Your grandfather could take his wife on a long drive on a winding road to a cabin with just the two of them for a few days. Better yet, he could let her drive with the top down in one of those sporty convertibles in some quaint town by the coast. But first, they could get coffee, muffins, or chocolate doodle things from a local bakery. Then, they could sit on the beach together. I think that would be quite romantic!"

Drew took Phoebe into his arms and proceeded to the deck. “Is my teasing bothering you? I have waited all day to be alone with you. I thought I could wait and give you something at your family’s home tonight. But I just couldn’t wait any longer, pretty lady. So, if you look in my right pocket of this shirt, I think you will find something that’s been waiting next to my heart all day.”

Phoebe looked up with her doe-like eyes. “Really? Right there?” she asked as she tapped outside Drew’s pocket.

“Yes, and he took her to his pocket. If you wait any longer, you’ll miss the dolphins, and I know how much you love dolphins.”

She smiled back. “That’s true. I love watching dolphins and sea turtles very much.” Phoebe looked into Drew’s eyes with her hands on each side of his face. “I love all God’s creatures.”

“You’re making this hard on me. Joe said Phoebe Farmer was that kind of woman!” Drew smiled.

Phoebe had a questioning look on her face. “Who’s Joe? How does he know what kind of person I am?”

“I met him in the church today. He said you were a lot like Ali and my mother. He told me I wouldn’t be able to hold on to you if I let go of God’s hand. I don’t want ever to lose you, so I agreed today. I wouldn’t let go because I never wanted to lose you.”

Phoebe cried. “I don’t want to let go of your hand. I don't want us to be separated, ever.” She looked in the pocket and opened the satin-wrapped box. It's beautiful. It sparkles so brilliantly," she spoke between sobs.

"I'm glad you said that!" I wanted it to have the same effect you had on me the first moment I saw you." Drew touched her chin and wiped off her tears.

"Oh really? I had a ponytail with no makeup on the first day you saw me."

"No. That wasn't the first time I saw you."

"What? Where did you see me before the day in the bakery?" Phoebe asked.

"Do you remember the picture you sketched of me wearing a toboggan?"

"Yes, I do. I found it on the internet with pictures of you when I learned who you were. I printed it off the internet." Phoebe stopped for a moment.

"Did you ever see the whole page from the newspaper article? It was a public relations piece about a local boy in the pros."

"No, I didn't. I was just looking for a sketch of you. I found the photo on the internet, and I liked it."

"That was my first year in the pros, and we played a team up north. The local paper printed a story about me. It came from one of the large newspaper networks. My mother bought several copies. There was another picture on that page as well. There were two beautiful women on a stage with a sash from the states they were representing. One was from Louisiana, my home state, and the other represented Maine. I knew the young lady from Louisiana. The beauty from Maine was the runner-up."

Phoebe looked at Drew with a stunned expression. "That was from three years ago."

Drew continued with his confession while caressing the braids in her hair. "The one with blonde flowing hair like this captured my heart. I even wished my team would trade to a team up there so our paths would cross. If I was going to sit on a bench, I could do it as well as the team I was on. What did a second-tier player on a team not going to the championship bring somebody who looked like you? I never expected that beautiful princess to be a sweet Georgia baker from Savannah."

"Drew, I'm taken by surprise by this revelation!" Phoebe said, trying to hold back sobs. "You are also ruining my makeup. I don't look like a beauty queen at this moment." Phoebe took a deep breath. "You need someone that has more than physical beauty. You are worth more than sharing your life with traces of gloss and highlighter. I almost lost myself in that world." Phoebe stopped for a moment and tried to push on. "Drew, you need to know something. I don't want to tell you now, though. It's in my mind again, but I don't want to recall it anything related to today. Can we be happy right now?"

"Then don't tell me now. I want to make you happy for the rest of our lives." Drew watched Phoebe's body language as she quieted down for a moment. He wiped her tears away with a tissue, then grabbed one rose and placed it in her hand. Let's walk outside and see if we see one of those creatures you love."

"Okay," Phoebe said and gave Drew the engagement ring to put on her finger. "That makes me happy."

"Me too." Drew slid the ring on to her hand, and before he took his congratulatory kiss, she pulled him outside and headed for the boat's bow. Drew grabbed a couple of blankets and hurried to keep up with her, tugging as they made it to the rail.

"The dolphins are already following us. There, see!" Phoebe pointed Drew toward the dolphins. There were two fins out there just above the water's surface, following the waves created by the boat. The elegant sea creatures leaped in the ripples as if they felt a sense of peace and vitality being one with their mate in nature. "I think they have been spying on us, wondering when you would make your move?"

"If you remember correctly, I started the play several weeks ago. I play offense, remember? So, you needed to catch that diamond on that pretty finger and complete my pass."

"Hmm, I can see it your way. I am more likely to let nature take its course. When I can no longer live without you, the spirit of who you are, I must accept my fate of walking with you. Our sea friends out there are our witnesses. I love them because they are here enjoying life with us."

"I don't know what all that meant, but I think it means you kind of like me a little." Drew teased and kissed her in the sunlight, noting her hair reflected illuminating light around her face from the golden strands they blew across her eyes and nose. Drew wrapped the small blanket around Phoebe's shoulders and put on his cap over her hair to protect her from the breeze and sun. He looked at her, eyes peeking at him from under the brim with the blanket up to her chin. He smiled to himself. Drew remembered a dream just like this scene before him with those beautiful violet eyes looking up at him. He thought to himself. Had he, too, been taken in by one of her magical ghost stories? This divine vision had tantalized his thoughts each night since the moment he saw her tugging on her ponytail and heard her say, "follow me."

Several hours later, Drew and Phoebe were within the city limits and away from the sea breezes. As the sunset had passed and the early evening hours were dark, the couple parked beside the Farmer's two-story traditional home. Thanksgiving tradition was underway. Holidays could mean crystal and candles. The fest was more informal in the last few years, allowing for an atmosphere of come as you are. Tonight, it was banquet-style on the screened porch. Tables were in the backyard, neatly done up with lanterns and white cloth. Glass jars were considered an acceptable drinking glass for iced tea and water. Mrs. Farmer placed the coffee, wines, and cider for after-dinner drinks with dessert on the sideboard. A walk or making chalk pictures on the driveway safely occupied the young children. By this point in the day, anyone over twenty needed a rest. A cushioned chair with an ottoman or porch glider was a coveted choice.

Drew and Phoebe sat on the Persian style floor cushions near Carole and Bob, Phoebe's grandparents from her mother's side.

"I'm glad you enjoyed being in the water today. All our kids have a special place for the ocean. I know I was hooked when Carole and I started dating. Her parents were already living on one of the surrounding islands. I was not much of a beach guy until I started coming here and spending time with Carol's folks. But then, it was the sea that called me. We always took outdoor vacations with the kids. Darla and Jesse love nature, which we tried to instill as a family value. Danny and Phoebe show a strong appreciation for the sea, but they are both from different generations, where there is much more to see and do. I understand that you've inherited your grandparents' home."

"Yes, I did. It's in excellent condition despite its age. It's quite a comfortable and unique place," Drew responded.

"Yes, it was always a little gem on that street. Charley and Ali would have kept the place up while they were living. Ali had a touch for decorating, and Charley was exceptionally good with his hands. It was not like him to have something big and grand. He would have valued comfort. Charley was an artist. Some people knew that, and some people never knew who he was. He was never just Reverend Howard. We went back to our college days. I didn't know Carole then, but I knew your grandmother. We were all friends back then. I never knew that Charley and Ali had something going on back then. I wish I could tell you more about your father. I didn't know Michael well. He died as a young adult. Charley never knew about Michael in all those years from what he told me. He loved your father very much when he found out. I can tell you from heart, Drew, he would be so excited to have his grandson and our granddaughter married. That would have delighted him. If he was here, I might even let him celebrate the scotch on the rocks with me. I have the bottle

I took from his house one night somewhere. That story is for another day."

Drew smiled at the older gentleman. "I bet there's an intriguing story you kept hidden with that bottle."

Bob shrugged his shoulder. "When you have as many miles on the tires as I have, Drew, there are many stories to tell. I do much else, but I sure have some stories to tell! If the time is right, I may share that story with you. But, of course, you may figure out that story on your own, like a puzzle, I would say."

"Dad, would you like me to put something in a box for you to take home? I already saved some of the German chocolate cake that you love. Drew, I have some for you too. That was one of your grandmother's recipes."

"Thank you, Darla, but I am leaving shortly myself, as we have practice tomorrow. It will be light, but I must check in before 10:00. That chocolate cake may not travel well with me."

"In that case, Drew, I'm making an order for your slices," Danny chimed in and gave Drew a tap on the back. "You must be aggressive in this family, Drew. My advice to you as a new member of the family is to put some muscle in it. If Mom says she has one bowl left of bread pudding and you want it, speak up. The gloves go on after that to determine the winner."

Drew laughed. "I will remember that."

"I have hand wrestled for the last chocolate cookie with this one, touching shoulders with his twin."

Phoebe twitched up her nose as she always did when she wanted to make a sarcastic statement, but then paused for a moment. “I am staying out of this. Danny is likely to spill some other ugly secret I am not ready to share with Drew on the day we are officially engaged.”

Silence filled the area for a moment. Drew chimed in to change the conversation back to Bob. “You know, I found a box of things that Ali left out at the house. I think she expected for me to see them when I arrived. I don’t know if you would have any information about them or not, Bob. Sometimes when I come back, we can look together."

Bob responded with a friendly pat on Drew’s shoulder. “I would be happy to help you put the pieces together. I’m probably the last one around who knew Charley the best. But I feel my lamp is ready to go out tonight, or I won’t be much good tomorrow. I never miss my Friday morning golf game, even if it is only nine holes. Remember, Drew; you must find time to be around the guys even when you’re married.”

“Dad, you said that from the earliest I can remember,” Danny said.

“Well, it’s true. Carole and I have been married for fifty-six years, and I have loved her for fifty-five of them. That was the secret to our beautiful life together.”

While working on her crossword puzzle, Carole remained quiet throughout most of the conversation. Finally, she stopped and put her pencil across the book. “Now wait a minute, fifty-five years! What year did you not love me, sir?” Carole looked over at her husband with her eyebrows raised and lips pursed.

"I don't remember exactly, but there must have been one terrible year in the mix because I remember needing to have my time with the boys a lot more somewhere in the middle."

"I see; well, in that case, I will excuse you because you lived to talk about it. That means you passed the skillet test. That, Drew, came as a testament to your grandmother Rona, a lovely woman. I haven't spoken to her in years. I will enjoy meeting them both again at the wedding. Phoebe, you may wish to ask for Rona's advice. She's a wise woman. Just wait until Drew and his grandfather aren't around." Her grandmother gave her a wink.

"I see I'm getting the poor boy in trouble already on the first day in the family," Bob said. "Carole, we should go home, so we don't break up the offspring before they even fly."

Drew, please do not make yourself a stranger. We would love for you to visit anytime."

"Dad and Mom, I will walk you out. Let me get your things in the kitchen."

"One more I would like to ask while you're here," Drew said. "Darla mentioned that the painting in the bakery was originally yours. Can you tell me anything about it?"

"Oh, let me think about that." Bob paused for a moment. "That is the one with Beaux, Charley's dog, in the loft?" "Yes," Drew responded eagerly.

"Yes, I was very fond of that one."

"Do you know anything more?" Drew asked.

"She didn't draw that. Charley sketched it. She was the painter in the family, but that was something that Charley drew."

Darla entered the room with a box of things for Carol and Bob to nibble on later. "I didn't know Charley drew that. I always thought Ali did. I guess I just assumed."

Bob responded, "No, that was Charley's work. When Ali came and brought Beaux, they were soon married. He made that sketch from memory of the first day Ali came to Savannah after the Christmas holiday. I'm not sure what happened when he went to see Michael, but it must have been an extraordinary week. Ali was living near Michael."

"I know about my father's house. I own it now, but I have not seen it. There is a tenant in the property," Drew added.

"Yes, I believe it originally came from Ali's side of the family. Unfortunately, I can't help you with that property, as I know nothing about it," Bob responded.

"Hopefully, we'll get to talk some more, Drew. I have forgotten some things over time, but your grandfather and I went back as far as our college days. That's when I met Charley and Ali for the first time. It would make them as happy as it makes Carole and me to have our families join the family tree. But I think Carole will have to whisk me off here before I become emotional and make a fool of myself."

"Yes, dear," Carole responded to her husband. She looked at Drew with a smile and winked. "Bob and I look good for our age, but there is much more maintenance now. We need to prepare for tomorrow's beauty today, or we won't be worth a dime tomorrow." The silver-haired couple walked together hand in hand to the car.

"Phoebe and Drew, congratulations!" Carole called out with a wave. "We'll be watching the game on Sunday!" The couple slipped into their sedan and started the motor

Darla watched her parents travel down the street to the next stop sign. "Mom and Dad are such a pair. Of course, they've slowed down some, but they still get around and do what they want."

"I want to be like them someday," Phoebe said with a smile.

"No, you don't, my sweet daughter. You want to be you. Your grandmother is exceptional, but even she will tell you she has some flaws. Small ones, of course, but she has them. That makes her the way she is, and your grandfather is the same way."

"You know Phoebe. I also need to leave. Can you drive me back to the house?" Drew asked.

"Of course, I will. I just wish you didn't have to leave." Phoebe responded and touched his chest.

"Phoebe, honey, is there anything you want me to pack up for you? I will be in the kitchen."

"Thanks, Mom. I'll be there in a minute to grab my purse and tell everybody goodbye. I don't want

this day to end."

"I know. I feel the same way. You could come back with me tonight," Drew responded.

"I know, but I have to tie things up here," Phoebe said. She barely heard her brother open the door behind them as she stared at Drew.

Danny took a step outside the door and interrupted the private moment. "Hey guys, I have an idea. Let me take Drew back to his place. You stay here with Mom and Dad for as long as you want. I'm closer to Drew's place."

Drew shrugged his shoulders and smiled back at both siblings. "That's fine with me," he responded graciously.

Phoebe looked over at Drew with some regret. "Yes, but..."

"Great. Shelly's going to drive the kids back in her vehicle. Drew can drive back with me in the truck so mom and Dad can talk about the birds, bees, and things before you go off and get married."

"Oh Danny, you're terrible!"

"It's a rite of passage in this family to hear the handed down family dos and don'ts before you ride off."

"Oh, Danny, you are making this all up in front of Drew to embarrass me. I will get even."

"Yes, I'm sure you will, but it works great this way. Drew's place is on the way home." He looked at the other two parties and responded, "Let me go back inside and tell the plan to the team and grab my keys." Drew went back inside and closed the door.

"We'll talk about everything when I get back to my house. But, please, don't keep me waiting much longer, Phoebe. I have thought about doing something desperate like kidnap and taking you to Iceland if you don't become Mrs. Drew Taylor soon."

"That's sweet. I won't make you wait," Phoebe looked at Drew earnestly. "I've made my mind up. You're the one for me. I know that to be true despite all your flaws, like being handsome and wealthy, having a grand piano in your living room, and driving that car! How could I drive a dump like that?" Phoebe blushed a little with that and giggled.

Drew smiled, and his face lit up, showing the tanned lines around his eyes. "I will trade in the convertible tomorrow."

"Not until I get to drive it once, okay!" Phoebe laughed with tears in her eyes. "I must make Lesley Ann Childes jealous just once, as she was the head cheerleader in high school, and she married the local high school football quarterback who is now the football coach at the local high school. However, after she sees me once in that thing, we'll be even for stilling my boyfriend right before the junior prom and leaving me without a date. Then, she and I can become chums again because I miss her as a friend, and I've held that against her since I was 16."

"Help me, Lord! I can see being married to you will drive me straight to church. You have pushed me to my limits already today!"

"Yes, but I'm the one for you, Drew. There is no argument from me anymore. I know it now, right here as she pointed to her heart. It's a sense of what is right. I want to sit down and talk with your grandmother. She sounds like a woman with wisdom," Phoebe responded with a smile. The door made a squeaky sound as it opened. Drew and Phoebe knew they were not alone.

Drew finished his thought. “That she does. Let’s get home so I can pack up and hit the highway.”

Danny cried, “I’m ready!” and started off to the truck. “I’ve got your coat. Great material. Was it bought in Colorado?”

Drew turned around and laughed. “It was!” He looked back at Phoebe and laughed. “Does he come with the package?”

“I’m afraid he does. We’ve been a pair since birth.”

“Got to love him!” Drew responded. He then leaned over to whisper in Phoebe’s ear. “You’re the air that my body needs.”

“It feels like that, Drew, but something else you're breathing is giving you a new life. I breathe it in too.”

Several minutes later, Drew and Danny were on the way eastward across the bridge and towards a surrounding chain of islands. Danny was a quiet at first. Then, finally, Drew started in with some questions.

“What relationship does Phoebe, or your family, have with the strawberry wine? You know I have about eight bottles right now.”

“Well, that sounds like you have a good year, then. Who gave you all those bottles?”

“I’m not sure exactly, but Phoebe was involved with the last bottle.”

“It’s not a big deal. We have a partnership in a wine-making business. The private-label version is an expensive wine. The business produces a limited volume each year, and the ingredients are premium, including the strawberries grown locally. We know the farmers, so we know how the strawberries are grown and treated. They know we care about our product, and they care for their plants."

"Like the ones we stop and buy at the market?"

"The same grower, but not the same berries. We have specific requirements for what and how we will buy from the farmer. The proceeds of what we make in part go to philanthropic projects. It is not a nonprofit. The investors get some return to keep them interested, but they also know that a portion goes to other projects that the board agrees to support. It's a privately held company, so we don't raise public funds." "Interesting. Is Rock Muffin somehow a part of this business?"

"Yes, he's one partner. He provided some necessary resources." Danny answered. He then looked at Drew with a face with no emotion, yet meaningful in his way. "Ian has known Phoebe since Maine."

Drew instantly became tense. "Since Maine? That's been a couple of years, at least."

"About that, a little more, actually," Danny responded as he put his foot gently on the brake at the bottom of the overpass, where a traffic light stood. "Phoebe's place goes that way." Danny pointed to the left. "Yours and my place go to the right at this intersection. You'll find that if you use that highway where the truck just turned on, it's a shortcut between the two islands, and you don't have to go back into the city and cross over on the bridge like we just did."

"Thanks." Drew paused for a few more seconds and then asked what was on his mind. "So, what about Ian and Phoebe? Did they ever date?"

"No." Danny did not elaborate further.

Drew knew he needed to know something that Danny knew, but chose not to tell it directly. "That's what he said, too. "Why do they seem to have a bond of secrecy between them?" Drew asked, trying to set Danny up for a response that loosened the seal of the family secret.

"He's a musician, songwriter type. He's not in town much. Ian has lived in the area for about three or four years in the section south of the city where many elite types live. You may even have some friends who live there, too."

"Yes, he knows my offensive coordinator. He plays golf with him."

"Yes, Sam, I've met him. Sam is a nice guy. I like him a lot from what I know of him. He's a good golfer."

Drew's inquisition would need to end soon as they were nearing the cottage that was becoming more than a property on a lot each time he returned. "I met Ian the other night at Jesse's place. He made a threat to break my arm if I hurt your sister. Never would I wish to do that. I feel certain he meant it literally."

Danny pulled into the lane next to Drew's car. He responded as he made a right turn into the drive. "I most certainly believe he would."

"I'm confused. Ian says he's never dated her, but he seems strongly protective of her. That usually only means one thing to me." "That's in the sometimes column," Danny said as he turned off the ignition. "Here you go, Drew, unharmed. Have a safe trip back. We'll keep Phoebe out of trouble until you come and claim her. Let us know if we can help you, okay?"

"Yes, Danny, I will most likely be in touch soon." Drew looked back at Danny, wondering if he had anything further to say. Danny said nothing more. Drew got out and went to the front door of the cottage. "Thanks again, Danny." Drew then turned the knob and walked inside. Strangely, it felt good to be here, and he would miss it when he pulled out to return to the crowded world awaiting him when he returned to the field of yards and goal lines.

Drew put his coat on the sofa and walked back to the bedroom. He washed his face, afraid that a shower may relax him too much and put him to sleep. His mind kept stewing about Rock Muffin as he remembered Phoebe's nickname when referring to the other guy by the sea with a European accent. The family seemed to have such a warm acceptance of the attention Rock gave Phoebe. Was he a potential suitor? Drew typically was never a jealous guy with women. However, Phoebe was different, and Drew felt uncharacteristically possessive. So why was the troubadour still singing outside the bakery window? Drew continued to mutter to himself while packing some things faster in his bag. *Thank goodness he wasn't Italian, or the odds of winning Phoebe dropped considerably,* Drew thought as he was demonizing Rock Muffin into his thoughts.

Thirty minutes later, Drew parked on the back side of Phoebe's white-painted home. Darkness had now set at this time of year. The lights told him she had not gone home to sleep, and that she had returned from her parents. Drew knocked on the door. After a few minutes, Phoebe came.

"You are supposed to be on the road back to the city." Phoebe stood with the door partially opened.

"Yes, I just need to talk to you about something. I need to know now, Phoebe. Please let me in."

Phoebe allowed Drew inside. "Okay, Drew. What's up? I thought you were on your way back." Phoebe created a path through the baskets of laundry sitting in the kitchen. Finally, Phoebe walked into the open living room space, plopped down on the lounge chair, and curled up, steering Drew to the sofa. "Can I get you anything?"

"No. No. I'm fine." Drew followed Phoebe to the sofa as directed. "I'm going to be straight with you." He looked at her face and didn't look away. She looked even more beautiful without makeup, if that was possible. "What does Ian McLoughlin mean to you?"

Phoebe put on a gentle smile but felt fear about where the conversation was going. "Drew, Ian is a friend, but it has nothing to do with our relationship." She looked at Drew with earnest eyes.

"I'm told you knew him when you were in Maine."

"Yes, I met him there," Phoebe responded truthfully. "I was a news anchor at a television station that was part of a larger network affiliate. I worked there briefly before the incident. One of my assignments was to interview the band Ian at the studio. After a sound check at the arena, we taped it in the afternoon before the band returned to their hotel. They were playing a couple of blocks away that night as headliners. That's when I met Ian"

"He's been hanging since that day. There's more to the story than meeting someone for an interview." Drew wasn't convinced that he was hearing the whole story. He had completed in enough interviews recently to know how the scene goes. The two hang around when there's a connection, and one calls or sends a text to the other. Then it's a meetup for dinner or a drink. "What was it with Ian, Phoebe?" Phoebe got quiet, and she hesitated to go on. "I know what you're thinking. Ian and I had a romantic relationship. Right?"

Drew shrugged his shoulders, but his eyes were black as coal. "I don't know what your relationship was with Ian. You tell me."

"That wasn't the case. There was never a romantic relationship."

Drew saw the uneasiness, but he knew he needed to know before returning. "Help me understand?"

Just then, Phoebe moved to unwrap her legs, and her robe came undone, exposing her right leg from mid-thigh down.

Unfortunately, her pink baby doll gown was too short to cover what she usually hid from anyone these days.

Drew noted the jagged line immediately. “What’s that?” he asked. Drew moved closer to her. His face was concerned as he moved closer gently to pull back the robe, exposing the scar down her leg. “Sweetheart, how did that happen?”

Phoebe's facial affect went flat as she let her guard down far enough to tell Drew the truth without feeling the pain of the scene all over again. “I accepted a job in New England was in the northern market was living in the Boston area after I graduated from college. My job was for a small satellite television station in one of the smaller communities. I hadn’t been there very long. A stalker seemed to follow me at home and near the station. Things kept happening, but I never saw the person, or at least I didn't know who it was. I knew someone was watching me and knowing where I was in my off time. I even contacted the police. I notified the police, but they couldn’t seem to follow the trail of things that happened. Finally, I decided, and my family agreed, that I needed to leave the area for my protection. My last day was on a Friday. Danny arrived Thursday and helped me pack the rental with all my stuff. He even had my car and planned to pick me up from work that Thursday.”

Phoebe took a big breath to hold back tears. “Danny had texted me to tell me he was at the light in front of the station. I started down the employee staircase to the door to the garage. I was going to stay inside until I saw the car. I finished the interview with Ian’s band about 30 minutes earlier. It was going to be taped and would air later that night. I guess part of his band went ahead in one car, and they were waiting on the second vehicle for Ian and the manager. A security person was staying with them. While waiting inside the building, someone came behind me, grabbed me, and pushed me through the door. I tried to run free, but I got pulled back again, and this time someone dragged me into the parking garage area. A cement wall hid the garage corner from the alley that separated the building and the garage. I screamed at least once. I don't know how many times I screamed. It was too terrifying to remember much afterward. Danny may have heard the first scream. I don't remember. The attacker heard someone beeping his horn and coming straight for us in the car. Before he ran away, he grabbed a glass bottle near his reach. He broke it and then cut my leg before he ran off. At some point, Ian and his entourage were coming out the back door, which was used for guests to keep their comings and goings private. He must have heard me scream. Ian told the limo driver to block the alley between the building and the garage and to get out with the keys. I understand he then pushed over a wheelbarrow and some field rocks in the alley, so if the attacker attempted to run that way, he would either trip on the rocks or get blocked by the car. The idea worked, and the security guard with him detained the guy until the other security people and police officers came.

"Did you know the attacker, Phoebe?" Drew asked gently.

She shook her head yes. "He was the television station's producer. He was the one who wanted to hire me when he met me at one of those social events during pageant week. I was so trusting and excited to be asked to be on television. But I was so caught up in all that stupid stuff about glamor and being a celebrity. It was so stupid of me. I shouldn't have walked down that lifestyle, focusing on beauty and celebrity and all that comes with it. I knew that. It was changing me, and I shouldn't have let it." Phoebe sobbed profusely at this point.

'That's why Ian is my friend and my family's friend. He helped me that day. Danny went with me to the hospital, and my mom and dad flew up the next day. Danny brought my things back. My mom, dad, and Uncle Jesse drove me back in a mobile camper, so I didn't have to bend my leg for the trip. They took turns getting me back to Georgia as fast as they could. Everybody tried to reduce the amount of scarring from an 18-inch jagged and gouged wound in my leg. The scar, you see, was the best we could hope for as she bared the shock to Drew.

From that day on, I was no longer a ballet dancer or the best swimsuit contestant winner. When I came back, it was a very dark time. It was Rock Muffin who inspired me to get up and do something. He pushed me back on my feet with his brief visits to love life again and stop living in self-pity. One night I was with people I knew better than hanging around. They weren't particularly beneficial influences, but I didn't care; I just wanted to be numb from pain, the heart kind. I was at the restaurant you saw Danny and me coming from the day we saw you. It was the night crowd, and I was with some people I rarely hang around, but they persuaded me to join them afterward for a few drinks and to listen to a band playing that night. Ian was there with some friends that night, too. I guess he had watched that I had a little more than I should have.

I was still behaving, but I think he was concerned that some things might change. He knew Myles, the owner, who was working in the back. Ian had Myles call Danny. Danny arrived and took me. Ian sat with me at a table until Danny got there. He said some things that felt like whiskey in a cut, but I won't ever forget what he said. Ian made inspired me to think I had worth again. He told me to visualize the most beautiful thing I could remember from childhood. It was about a mermaid who lived near a beautiful island from a book that Uncle Jesse bought me. That's why Uncle Jesse still uses that nickname for me. By the time Danny went there that night, Ian had me thinking of a world that existed before the attack.

"So that's how Ian McLoughlin protected you." Drew put his fingers through Phoebe's hair and gently massaged her head and shoulders. I guess I've been making a fool of myself by being jealous."

Phoebe nodded. "There's only friendship between us. I thought he would ask me out, and I won't say that I don't have some attachment to him as he was there when I was hurting. However, there's nothing more." Phoebe paused for a moment and smiled to lighten up the story. "He has several women in his life. I guess I'm just not his taste."

"Well, he must have poor taste. Drew tried to make Phoebe laugh to release the pain she had been carrying since the attack. "I suspect your Rock Muffin has been around enough to be tempted by all kinds of land and sea creatures. Even alligators let the snowy egrets be during the day while they sleep on the banks of lagoons and pools of water near the sea. Bears do the same in Alaska with the birds as they land near the salmon prey along the river and falls. The rangers say it's all those bones and no meat on them and not being a tasty morsel to bite into when one is a hungry beast. He had enough sense to inform you that you are still a beautiful woman. There is no mermaid to compare to you. I am your protection from today forward. How about me staying right here tonight? I will put you back in your bed and sleep right here. I will text the team coaches to say that I will arrive before noon, but I may not meet at the 10:00 AM meeting, depending on when I leave. You are in my safekeeping tonight and for the rest of our years together. Got that!" Drew kissed Phoebe's nose.

A short while later, Phoebe crawled into bed, pulling the white down comforter up to her chin. She quickly fell asleep, free of the burden she had carried in the dark corners of her heart for the last three years.

Drew sprawled his body over the white canvas upholstered sofa. He pulled up a cover around himself to ward off the slight chill. Drew picked out the fabric pattern in the dim light, revealing pink dolphins and starfish in a background of cream. He smiled to himself. Big Cid would never know that his signal caller wrapped himself up in pink sea creatures the night before the big push for the most challenging team they faced this season.

When the clock showed 2:00 in the morning, Phoebe stirred. She heard a movement in the living room and recalled the events of the day before. She felt her finger, and the ring was still there. It wasn't a dream. She crept under the warm cover and picked the brush off the nightstand. She walked to the archway in the door and leaned against the door frame.

Drew looked up and smiled back. "I didn't want to wake you, but I thought I might do the first practice if I left early enough."

"Yes, that's good. I don't want the team to hate me for keeping you away from the football field."

"It was worth it," Drew said as he walked over to her.

"Are you all packed up and ready to go?" Phoebe asked.

"Yes, it looks like it."

Phoebe looked around and reached out for Drew. "Will you come dance with me.?"

Drew looked over at Phoebe, knowing there were few things he would not deny her. "Absolutely," he whispered.

She took his hand and led him to the decking facing the house's ocean side. "I haven't danced with a partner in three years. Please dance with me in the moonlight before you go."

Drew held her body on the porch as she moved her scarred limb into her silken gown. Drew looked at the sky as he nuzzled his chin against her head. One star glowed larger than the rest.

"I thought of a date."

"And?" Drew asked.

"I want to be married the first weekend in February; the interviews are wrapping up for the season, and I will have more of you to myself for at least a few weeks until it starts again. Then, I want to celebrate the coming of spring and a gift larger than anything we could have built, earned, or bought." When Drew didn't respond, she looked up and followed Drew's gaze. "It's beautiful, isn't it?"

"Yes, the first weekend in February is perfect," Drew murmured back, not comprehending everything she had said. "Yes, the star is beautiful. He felt Phoebe's body move to the gentle sound of the tide coming in, and it reminded him how much he didn't want to leave. "That the star shining largest seems to follow me, or maybe I'm following it."

"Yes, Drew," Phoebe said and pulled herself away. She gently retook his hand and led him inside. It was time for him to return to his world.

Chapter 6

"It looked like you were having fun out there today, Drew," the sports reporter asked as she pushed the microphone in Drew's face.

"It's always fun when the entire team plays well. The guys worked hard throughout the week. It was a good day." Then Drew quickly hustled back through the tunnel. One more game closer to the playoffs. That was the buzz in the locker room. He checked to ensure a particular box was in his locker and did the next interview. Yes, it was there. It was becoming like a lucky sock or shirt. Don't let it stop coming, or he knew his luck would stop. He read all the congratulatory texts once he got home. It feels much better this December than last December, he had to admit. He then read Phoebe's text. How about California, a Tuscan-style villa with a courtyard in the wine-making region, brunch after the wedding in the wine-tasting room with authentic barrels? A magazine wants to do an article and photograph the wedding?"

Drew left a voice mail this time and stated it sounded great. He'd call her in the morning and find out more. *I'm missing your voice.* The tough guy in the locker room admitted. He shook his head, longing for more than the sound of her voice. He was happy that she was still saying "yes" to him. *How could anyone but an angel or a devil agree to this circus of life he lived?* He had another emerging issue as he went through a few more messages. He needed to block out some time to talk to somebody tomorrow. Cid or Sam, he wasn't sure whom he needed to speak with, but something was pushing on his thoughts. If something pressed harder than football, he knew he had to address it.

Before another 10 minutes had passed, he texted back to Phoebe again. Are you sold in California? I have another idea. I will call you tomorrow morning before the shop opens. Hold the phone next to the oven. I want to smell your fresh croissants while I'm sipping my coffee.

The following day brought on new checks on his due list and a bit more responsibilities. Drew was having the time of his life. Every bruise and ache verified he was alive from the inside out. That's where his energy came from these days. No longer was he on the bench, but working out of the playbook he was reading and memorizing these days. He admitted it was harder to deal with the blindsides. Drew took his offensive coach's words to heart after the last game.

Sam just smiled at him when he talked about the tough ones. "Preparation is a must. Be prepared to use what you know.

Do your job with your tools: quick release, aim, distance, and scramble on those feet. The team's receivers have to do their job with their talents. Listen to the coach. He's got the map of the bigger picture. Keep the noise out of your head!"

Drew reflected on the message. Did Sam mean decibels or thoughts? Drew had some control over that. He called some contacts to remove the noise he carried that was loading him down. One of those calls he felt pressed to make was to his grandparents. *The lion couldn't be ignored much longer*. Grandfather Robichaud had been waiting to hear something since Thanksgiving. Drew didn't have an answer for him yet. The next game was all he had thought about since the last conversation. The dilemma was another game kept popping up with each win.

A few weeks later, the division leader was the team that Drew wore the jersey for each week. The team had made it through to the next round. The injury list contained sprained ankles, torn ligaments, bruised ribs, concussion, and broken toes, along with several minor injuries. Drew laughed when he saw his team Jake make the list. Drew knew the background of the injury, not specifically stated on the list.The true was that one of the large defensive tackles received a bitte on the left buttock caused by a donkey from one of the petting zoos in the area. Jake went back into a stall that he thought was empty when he tried to duck around the corner from his ex-girlfriend as he was with his new girlfriend, her child, and one on the way. The thing was, Jake loved children and loved animals. Typically, he would have been prepared for the situation. However, fear took over the 6-foot 4-inch kicker when the scene involved two female adults wearing the armor of false lashes and designer shoes converging at the exact coordinates in less than 90 seconds. Jake took a desperate escape route to the mouth of a third female of a different species. Luckily enough for Jake, it was just a flesh wound. However, the injury made the weekly list, as it disturbed his kicking aim. The very well-intentioned athletic trainer offered a soft cushion. However, the young man made a fast dash from Jake's left hook when a meaner than Beelzebub's expression was on the kicker's face.

Drew's mind was struck with a blindsiding message after practice the day after Christmas. The coach told Drew that the first-string quarterback's medical checkup would determine his eligibility to be removed from the injured reserve list. What did that mean for Drew, who was now looking forward to the playoffs? He rested his tired body on the lounge chair on the first floor of his home, looking out into the closing darkness after sunset. He was going to be married as soon as the season was over. Drew wanted to have time off mentally to enjoy this moment with the love of his life. He would have to wait till February since it looked like the team would enter the playoffs, but he didn't want to wait anymore. Football always came first since he was in middle school, when people started seeing him as having a future career in sports. His life followed a strict recipe. School nights were practice or games, and there were few social nights or vacations. Drew stopped for a moment and remembered his time with Grandpa Howard before he passed. Those were his most cherished moments. Charley was never in a hurry. Yet, he packed in so much, living in each moment in his older years. Phoebe's grandfather and Charley were a perfect pair of opposites and teammates, living out their lives in a way they felt called. Drew thought fondly of both. Add CeCe's dad to the list in the mix, and there was a group of men that could cause something big to happen. Drew heard the stories as a young boy while sitting with the other two men on Charley's boat. Drew agreed that the best stories are with a reel, bate, and a cold beverage in the ice chest. He experienced the camaraderie of friendship and tales with the three men on a boat, oblivious to the young boys in earshot while they shared their ideas and secrets. One day, those boys would grow up and understand that some of the most significant decisions happen in these brief moments. Drew recalled Charley always brought root beer for Drew and Danny. It was a treat, as root beer wasn't as available in this part of the south. Charley would sip the tea Grandma Ali made for him fresh each day from a thermos. Bob and Richard preferred the more potent brew when they docked. But out in the waterways, they would pop the can on whatever generic brand Carole would pack in the cooler. If it was cold, nothing compared to an orange or clear fizzy drink, according to the wise words of Bob.

Drew amazed himself that he could still remember the details from the few days he spent with those men. Then, his mind returned to his thought of Phoebe as they often did. *What was Phoebe doing right now? Was she saving her turtles at the sea turtle hospital? Drew's sweetheart thought of her trying out a hairstyle for the wedding. In his mind, he hoped she left it down. He loved the silken strands against his face. But then Drew's mind went darker. What if she was planning to make a box of chocolate cakes and deliver them to Rock Muffin in the morning?* That box should be for me! Drew immediately took out his phone and texted his mermaid—*Miss you and the chocolate things that smell so good and feel so soft in my hands.*

Drew's phone blew up within seconds. He read the text. *The coach says no, tempting his quarterback until the big game. I am counting the days until the gloves come off! Also, do you like purple or blue?*

Drew thought about the question for a second and replied,

I have purplish-blue marks all over my body. I think I would like something a little sunnier.

A few seconds later, a new text came over his phone. It read:

I didn't think of that. Okay, sunnier it is. I liked that one too! Sending you kisses to make those bruises go away!

♥

Chapter 7

DREW STOOD ON THE sides of the practice field with the coach and the offensive coordinator. The big decision before the last playoff game was now, as there wasn't any time. Sam told Drew that Bozeman received a clean bill of health. "We want you to know that, but we also want you to know we are starting you on Sunday. You brought us to the dance, and we're going to show you we believe in you by giving you this shot. Those men in front of you have been listening to your signals most of the year. The receivers feel the rhythm and find their spots on the field to make the connection. We don't want to mess with a good thing." Sam smiled, but his eye showed steely confidence that he meant what he said.

"Thanks. I appreciate your support. We are going to win. It's not for me; it's for the whole bus that follows us from September through January."

"I believe you!" Sam spun around and shouted out. "Now, rest up. It's showtime on Sunday!" All trotted off the field and into the dressing rooms.

As Drew made his way out of the facility, Bozeman caught him on the way out.

"Hey, Drew. I know about Sunday. You're going to make it happen, Drew! I know you will. Look what you've done this year."

"Thanks, man. I didn't want to get my shot this way."

"That's the way life is sometimes. I didn't realize that they could rehabilitate me at this point. I believe the One above has the plan; best not fight it."

"Yep, you're right." Drew had liked Bozeman as a person but spent little time away from football, getting to know him personally. Strange, he thought, as he should have known Jake the most of anyone on the team. Teammates spend so much time together that they are like brothers. However, Drew knew little of the man out of the uniform. He knew he liked to write music. Cid said he is good. Drew would make it a point to pay more attention the next time his teammate brought out his guitar. "You don't talk about your faith much. I wish I understood it all more," Drew said without knowing those thoughts were in his head.

"That's a good thing, Drew. Just like in football, hunger is a good thing. It drives a person to search and dig to find out what it all means. We need to spend some time on the golf cart together. If I'm not good at sharing what I know, my driving will put the fear of God in you!" Bozeman said with a laugh. He gave Drew a pat on the back. "Let's go home. I have three princesses and one six-month-old bulldozer with floppy ears waiting for me there. I hear you are engaged to a golden hair angel to look out for you. He takes loving care of us, Drew. He knows whom to put in our world at the right time."

Drew made it home after practice on Friday, looking forward to spending a few hours with Phoebe before the cycle started back in the morning for the big game on Sunday. She had arrived late Thursday night to spend the weekend going to the playoff game on Sunday, given that it would be on the home field. A note with a smiling face sat on the counter when he arrived.

I will be back soon. I made some new friends today, and they wanted to show me around. Phoebe

He smiled, thinking of Phoebe fluttering around the kitchen while he was at practice. He wanted to watch her drink her morning mix of sludge while he sipped his coffee at the table on the balcony. There she would be with her overstuffed sweater with her hair pulled into a ponytail. He loved the look of a little black dress and red lipstick, but her natural beauty provided him comfort like a bowl of gumbo after Christmas Eve mass. Soon they would be married after the season, and they could share their time by the sea. For now, he had to accept her brief visits. She had already reconnected with one of her old pageant comrades, who was a wife to the other team's defensive lineman. The two ladies sat together at the game on Sunday in a neutral box that an international beverage distributor offered. Drew shook his head again as he looked at her signed note. He questioned himself. When is it my turn? Just then, Drew heard the door downstairs open. He thought he heard something strange. "Oh no! She didn't." Drew cringed.

"Drew, I'm back!"

He heard that feminine voice and knew she wasn't alone. *This was what his safe, quiet life would be like from here on out.* Drew sighed as he hurried downstairs to meet his guests.

A few hours later, Drew found himself nestled in the surroundings of two blondes. The one had herself nestled under his arm, while the second had its nose pressing against his ribs as he petted the little pug with his left hand. All three lounged on the sofa.

"Drew, you didn't ask me what you think of me keeping my partnership in the bakery or giving up my ownership completely."

"Humm..."

"That's not an answer!"

"No, but it is all the response I want to give tonight. It's your decision. I am enjoying the most delectable evening after a tiring week. I don't want to steer my mind away from anything but the moment."

"All right then, I'm going to keep my share for now, but I want to have an understanding that I will most likely continue my involvement." Phoebe made a slight movement, and the pug countered by nudging closer to Drew's palm for more attention. "I wish Monica and Ben could stay for dinner tomorrow, but I understand how this works. It's so hard to have friends be your competition. Yikes, I'm going to have to learn so much. I don't know if I can even fit in."

"First, you are already making friends. That's not your weakness. My second point is that there is the off-season which allows for more interaction. The season is so tight that there is not much time for socialization that somebody does not direct. Finally, I never want you to be anything other than yourself. This game can ruin some people because many things pull the players and their families in different directions. My reward is getting to know the real you. I never want you to change."

"That sounds nice, but I want to change, Drew. I don't want to be somebody I'm not, but I want to become more compassionate and generous and have all the qualities I believe God has for me. I'm a canvas not finished."

"You and me both." Drew kissed Phoebe on the head and continued to look forward. He saw the firelight on the right while he watched the evening sky. Just beyond his view was a brilliant star twinkling in the heavens above. There it hovered overhead, as if it was listening.

Game day arrived, and Drew had already left to join the team. Phoebe and Monica had joined up and followed the directions given to join their host for the afternoon. The two social butterflies were in their element, enjoying meeting people and conversing on diverse topics before the game began. Once the game started. Phoebe centered her attention on the one player who called the signals. She twisted her scarf, and at other times, she jumped out of her chair. By the second quarter, she needed to do something besides watching behind the glass while her insides churned. Finally, halftime arrived, and Phoebe slipped away. Before she returned, she stopped in one of the network boxes and watched intently on a monitor. When she saw what she wanted, Phoebe thanked the gentleman she had spoken with and rushed back to take her seat again. By the end of the third quarter, Phoebe felt mixed emotions. Another game looked likely and another delay to their plans as a couple.

The game was Drew's mission. At the end of the fourth quarter, and the points continued to be higher on the home team than on the opponent's side. The team added another big game into Drew's season. Congratulations spread joyfully around the team's locker room. However, Drew kept the disappointment shuttered in his heart and beneath the charming smile.

The events of the day still shocked Drew when he got home and settled in for the night. Many of the guys were still probably celebrating. Drew went to celebrate with Phoebe and the new family member before she left for her return to Savannah. He sat and watched the game replay from a couple of news outlets. When he turned the channel again, he stopped when he saw a familiar face on the screen. There was the little boy he had met before Thanksgiving in Savannah. Drew turned the station up. According to the reporter, the youth, after being given tickets for the game.

One boy chimed in and said he was wearing his lucky hat so the home team would win. The boy reported disappointment that his friends didn't believe him and that he got the cap from a real football player. He beamed with a big smile on the camera and said to the reporter, "At halftime today, someone came by and gave us all t-shirts to wear. Then a vendor brought hotdogs and drinks for all of us. My friends believe me now!"

Bishop Franks added, "The community helped support this outing for these boys, and he wanted to thank everyone who made it happen as it was a memory they would never forget."

Drew sat back on the sofa just as he did the night before when his arms were full of bundles of joy and soft trouble. He smiled to himself and texted Phoebe. Did you get me a T-shirt? LOL, #5.

Five minutes later, he got a text back. *Got it on*. Bring your brawny arm and wrestle me for it. LOL

The following two weeks of preparation for the big show were intense. One goal drove Drew's focus each day. He was in his performance zone. Those in his circle knew he was not in the decision or planning mode for anything but the big game.

Phoebe respected these boundaries, but it felt the loneliest since she began the relationship with Drew. For the next two weeks since she returned to Savannah after seeing Drew play, she had felt the intensity of being separated from love. Nothing met the hunger Phoebe had in her heart. She wanted it to be like when they first met. Drew had been in the off-season then. She tried to smell the saltiness of mixed sweat as they jogged along the beach and marshes together. She remembered the night she danced in his arms, hearing the tide rush in and the breeze touch her limbs as she moved on the porch with the ocean in the background. Stored in her memory was the vision of him in his crisp white shirt and tan pants when he first walked into the bakery. Phoebe wanted the man out of his uniform and into the clothes he wore when he was just being Drew. I want back. She sipped her tea and looked out through the windshield. She sat in front of his cottage on Willow Way. The season would finally be over when she returned from the west coast. She and Drew could finally be home together. With wishful thoughts, she picked up the soft, squirming puppy with all his toys and walked to the house next door. Uncle Jesse was there to receive the bundle while Phoebe was away.

"Junior and I will get along fine, Phoebe. Have a fun and safe trip. Myles is bringing in a large screen for the social hall that Danny was renovating. So that's where we will be for the game. It's going to be fun on Sunday."

"Yeah, tell Myles we appreciate all his support! I need to go to catch my flight. I will see you when I get back."

"You bet. Bring that fellow home, and we'll do it right with a shotgun wedding!"

"Love you!" Phoebe said as she hugged her uncle and walked to the car.

It was Saturday night before the last game, the one that mattered. And Drew was alone in the hotel room. It was now 10 o'clock on the east coast. Drew wondered what Phoebe was doing now. He thought of her curled up against her pillow. He didn't want to disturb or keep her while she slept, so he wouldn't try to call. She had an early flight out in the morning. Less than ten days away, she would finally have Taylor for the last night. He couldn't think about how much he missed her or would feel the pain, which didn't match his mission right now. He couldn't let the guys down or allow them to know he had a weak spot right now. Drew thought he would have more time to develop the relationship when he first met her, given his history in professional football. Nobody paid that much attention to the second-string football player. By now, the season should have ended for the team. Drew would be blissfully putting sunscreen on her back or having a little barbeque in the backyard, with her floating around in her little sundress. He missed her influence. He missed her joy. Drew missed her touch. She went away to live with the bakery's smells and among the turtles and starfish. She was gone and left him behind. Drew felt the pressure of needing to find the way home. He envisioned the outer man as a ghost that returned to the pig skin he tossed around each day and proceeded with the routine. Without Phoebe, Drew felt lost in his world. He placed his head in his hands. *What is happening to me?* Drew stewed in his frustration. After half an hour had passed with no relief, Drew picked up the phone and called someone else who might be up. He was ready to talk.

Chapter 8

THE BIG GAME HAD arrived. The usual circus of media, vendors, and spectators set up their spots hours before kickoff. Drew's mother and stepfather were in town and met with Drew briefly last evening at the hotel after dinner. They stayed with friends and planned to come together as a group for the game. Phoebe was also here for the game, but was more secretive about her location. She would be in an unfamiliar area with some of the team's wives, including Sam. Drew was glad about that, as he didn't want to worry about her being alone. Lately, Sam figured out Drew's prayers to God. Drew never thought of Sam as the angelic sort, but recently the man had grown some wings in his eyes. Drew had to accept the idea that God made many creations. It shouldn't be so far from the truth that God needed some sailor-swearing brutes to keep some of his creations in line. He hated mean-spirited people. However, he could respect a bear of a personality who had a good heart under it all. Drew guessed that was what Sam's wife saw in him.

Drew hoped Phoebe saw the same goodness in him, even when he wasn't so perfect.

The uniforms were on. The players had come with their game faces. What preparation looked like for each of the players was a unique story. They were all there to win. Drew looked around, sizing up the opponent as he stood with his team as they announced the players. The other team's quarterback did the same. Drew warmed up his arm along the sidelines. His thoughts reviewed a script of himself being the leader in this situation. *I have prepared for this. I know how to move the ball on this field. I can release the ball faster than they can reach me. My feet know how to move this body anywhere I want to go. I can throw and hit my target to the left, to the right, and down the middle. I will give my best* at *each play.*

The play began with a coin toss, causing Drew's team to receive the kickoff. The leather ball moved up the field and into the opponent's territory for the next several plays. However, a field goal would be all they would get on the first drive toward the goal post when Drew returned to the sidelines.

Sam was there to pump him up. "Play your game, Drew. They don't know all your plays. The other team is feeling you out right now. They don't know you as I know you. You have prepared for this game all season. The left defensive tackle is a gigantic wall, but he's slower than your offensive arsenal. Catch him looking the wrong way; your man is through the center. He likes predictability to plug up the holes with his body."

Drew took to the field in the second quarter, running the game evenly at ten points for each team. A field goal attempt was good by the opponent seconds before halftime to increase their score to thirteen. It only made him more determined as he walked into the tunnel than the underdog. He was determined to play his best, whatever that took. As he sat near his running back while in the locker room, Drew overheard Raj say that this was the first game his father had attended a game in his son's professional career. Maintenance people at hospitals work seven days a week. Raj's father would have his wife record the fun, and he watched the game after he got off from his second shift. He would make notes and roll them back if he saw something the referees didn't catch. Raj's dad would email the messages to Raj each week. The assistant thought Raj's father was in the second group of chairs about twenty rows in the stadium from their bench, as he spotted a shirt with Raj's number on it. Drew felt the tug of how proud Raj's dad must be today. He wished he could see his parents and Phoebe in the stands today, but that was something he couldn't concentrate on while playing. Finally, he got Raj's attention and said, "Remember paintball! When I say it, do you know what to do? Be prepared in the fourth quarter if we get to the forty." Drew talked some things over with the coach and the guys. Finally, they were ready to take the field. It was going to be a hard-fought game to the end.

The third quarter continued to be a close matchup, with both teams adding a touchdown. By the end of the third quarter, Drew and the offense had moved the ball close enough to earn another field goal tying the game. Nobody was leaving for the buses yet. A few terrible calls got a roar of boos from the opponent's fans. The referees received cheering in the section where Phoebe and Drew's parents sat. The fans of Drew's team wanted a win. That was noise to Drew; he turned it out while mentally pushing harder through each play. He would end up watching it on replay repeatedly after the game. Drew left the field with less time on the clock for one more fourth down. No time to stew about it now.

Sam jogged over to where Drew was standing. "Knock out the noise, Drew. What do you hear on the inside? That's whom you listen to now!"

Drew looked into Sam's steely gray eyes and calmed himself by trying to listen to the quietness of the calming voice inside. Then, finally, the barrage of sounds from the stands and the field went silent. He looked at the stands filled with fans behind the players' bench, and with determination, he took to the field with his fighting warriors when it was their turn to charge toward the goalpost again.

Deep into the eighteen-yard line, Drew focused on moving the team in increments across the field. He forced the offense line closer to the fifty-yard line with short passes and rushing plays that were just enough to get those extra few yards to turn it over to first down. The opponent's defense line became more expansive and taller with each first down Drew's team gained. They were now less than halfway to the goalpost. Drew made quick decisions on his feet to move the ball closer to the target. They were not in excellent field goal range from the forty-five-year line yard line. Get me to the forty-yard line. Drew kept concentrating on the throw. The plays came in from the sideline, but the one that mattered most was the one Drew was ready to call. Paintball moved the leather object down after Drew threw a quick pass to the left. Raj made it past the thirty-yard line, then the twenty, and into the 10. Raj had reached the end zone. Drew met Raj coming off the field.

Raj looked at Drew with tears in his eyes. Dad was watching! He watched the whole thing!"

"I know! You gave him something to brag about to all the folks back home!"

Drew gave him another hug. Again, he felt the comforting message in the tiniest part of his heart. Drew became teary-eyed and whispered, "My Dad was watching too."

The photographer on the sidelines snapped the shot of the two men talking helmet to helmet. It captured the winning moment of the game regardless of the final score.

When the last whistle blew to end the game, the points on the Georgia team were higher than that of the other team. As one would expect, there were high-fives and hugs. The boys picked up the coach and carried him to the podium. Reporters swarmed around the players to conduct the interviews. Sam's wife had found a way for Phoebe and Drew's parents to follow her to the field near the tunnel entrance. As Drew moved closer, he spotted them and headed toward them, jogging with several camera operators and reporters following him. CeCe was the first to hug her son.

"Your father would be so proud, Drew. I could feel him being here with us."

"I know, Mom, I felt it too!" Drew tried to be polite and acknowledge those passing him by who were congratulating him. However, he felt the press of others directing him toward the tunnel and the locker room beyond.

Drew looked at Phoebe and hugged her with no words coming out at first. "I'm still that man on the bench, but I found a burning bush that put a fire in me," Drew finally got out. "You led me to this wild adventure. It reminds me of the mountain fairies in your tale of being lost in the winter. I love your stories, and I love Uncle Jesse's mermaid!"

Chapter 9

DREW RETURNED TO THE city a few days after returning from the west coast. He had a mission. Before Phoebe, Drew had never set out to woo a female. All the women he had known had fluttered around him like butterflies. The guys he spent time with knew the picture well. Not until Phoebe had Drew become the seeker. Drew had to be honest and realize that something unexpected happened to him along the way. The hunter changed during the chase. It made him appreciate the sentiment that what he hunted for eventually changed him. He wanted Phoebe to be the vibrant living being that he loved. This was someone he wanted to share his days and nights with for the rest of his life.

When Drew pulled into the drive at Willow Way, people were already in action. He could tell that a rental car was in the drive. His family members were arriving, it would seem. His mother, stepfather, and the Robichauds would stay in the main house tonight. Drew would sleep in the studio this evening. The night before the wedding and Drew would celebrate at dinner with both families present. The night before the wedding.

Phoebe had planned not to see Drew until this evening, as she had much to do. She even stopped texting back after twelve.

In Drew's eyes, a little jog on the beach for training past her little cottage was not entirely out of line. However, when he tried that maneuver. He saw no one was there. Someone had drawn the blinds, and there was no sign of activity. How did that minx know he would try to peek he wondered? As he moved closer, he saw a note on the French door from the ocean side. His curiosity won out, and he pattered through the soft sand of the shore to cross over to near the wraparound porch. When Drew looked closer at the sign on the door, familiar handwriting peered back at him with a smiley face stuck on the stationery.

She will see you this evening. Rona.

He turned back around, realizing he was in deep water now and didn't mean high tide! Drew muttered as he passed the pelican watching him from a post a few feet away. The clan has descended, and the female members are in control. *They are protecting my little dove,* Drew thought to himself. The pelican moved his head at an angle as if he was listening closely. Drew looked at the bird in frustration. "You are probably working with them, aren't you? You can fly back and tell them I know they're good naturedly scheming, but I have Grandfather Robichaud on my side, and we can outsmart all of you!" A few seconds later, the pelican took off over the sea and toward the inlet of the Savannah River.

Drew went back the way of the road to the parking lot as a shortcut. He knew he needed to put on armor now. Drew knew capturing a moment with his lady wouldn't be easy. He had fished with a net when he was young with his Grandpa Charley from the dock. He just had to be patient now.

Thirty minutes later, Drew was in front of the bakery. He parked and walked inside, only to be greeted by Uncle Jesse, who was closing the shop. Someone had already placed a custom sign in the window announcing they would be closed for the weekend. One corner of the plaque displayed silver bells.

Drew also noted an empty spot on the wall in the shop as he peeked in to see if anyone else was inside. He wasn't sure what that meant, but he was picking up signs that both families were kidnapping Phoebe until the family dinner. Drew signed and realized he should have expected this game because he left females out of the location plans when he canceled California as the option. Phoebe only needed to pick out her dress, colors, and menu selections given to her by an anonymous assistant. Drew provided Phoebe with instructions that allowed her to make a list of things that she had to have at her wedding. Drew would pass the information on. They would incorporate the items if possible. He chuckled when Charlotte told him Phoebe had written "groom" on the returned list and then crossed it off. Phoebe wrote *Optional next to the crossed-out entry for the groom.* He knew Phoebe had put that down, as she knew it would get back to him. Drew had to inform some of the family members of some details, but only when necessary. He realized now that Phoebe and her companions had arranged for this payback! It was finally 5:00 PM, and the cottage belonging to Drew was busy with the loading of vehicles. Steven and his wife rode with his parents in a special van for the weekend.

Drew preferred to ride alone, hoping Phoebe would ride back with him. The Farmer side would meet them at the designated location. His family followed drew as they reached the drive that led to a white two-story inn that housed a fine dining restaurant that sat over a bluff. Cars arrived one after the other, with Phoebe and her parents arriving last. A staff member guided the arrivals onto the side patio while waiting for the last car. The ladies received a rose from the inn's owner as he mingled among the guests, awaiting the last arrival.

Drew had anxiously waited for this moment all day. He recalled the first moment he met her at the bakery and had matched the face with the photo he had seen in the newspaper with a picture of Miss Maine. He would have never dreamed of finding her in a coastal town he had visited as a child. But her broken wing brought her back home. Finally, his wounded heart brought him to hear his angel's prayers.

Phoebe's smitten beau watched for her as her proud father, Ryan, escorted her from the car. After walking halfway up the sidewalk, he patted his daughter's hand, knowing her future husband desired to take her the rest of the way. Darla and Ryan walked hand in hand.

Drew stopped to grab the remaining rose from the box, presented it to Phoebe, and kissed her hand. For a moment, he was speechless. She was the divine image of everything he could hope for in a mate. Striking fuchsia silk, clothed her; the sleeves were off the shoulders, and the formfitting lines created a pencil skirt that reached just above the knee. She had drawn her hair to one side in cascading blonde curls, falling over one shoulder. Drew loved everything he saw and wanted to remember this vision forever. He could feel the heat she radiated when he put his hand on her back to usher her further inside. He whispered in her ear.

Phoebe smiled back and whispered back. She blushed when she saw his smile.

Drew touched her lips. "How did I stay away this long?" He soaked in everything about her. He took in the fragrance, the color of her lipstick, and the shape of her kneecap as it peeked below the hemline.

Your mother helped me pick out which dress I should wear. She also gave me something to wear tonight. Phoebe took a little box from her clutch. She said your father gave it to her the night before they were married. Would you put it on for me?"

Drew opened the small box and took out the dainty diamond pendant on a delicate chain.

"It's perfect for you," Drew whispered as he took the necklace, opened the clasp with his long fingers, and placed it around Phoebe's neck.

"Thank you, Mother. Your gift means a lot to both of us." He kissed CeCe on the cheek.

Drew's attention again returned to his bride-to-be. He could see the natural gift she possessed. He saw her inner beauty deepen in layers as he drew closer to her. She was flesh and blood and ethereal at the same time. Drew had seen her beautiful before in summer shorts and a t-shirt. But she was the brilliant diamond this evening.

She reached for his arm and gently kissed him before nudging Drew to follow Ian's cue and gather the family to begin the celebration.

Once the group assembled, Ian McLaughlin, the inn's owner, guided them inside to the dining area, which the staff had arranged with floral arrangements and lit candles on each table. Finally, he bid the group goodbye and left the building quietly through the back entrance. A capable staff, well trained to make the evening a beautiful experience for the entire party, would handle everything.

A few minutes later, Drew whispered something in her ear when he guided her to a chair along a long, formal dining table. Phoebe held back a blush.

Rona looked over at the other matriarch in the family, smiled, and winked. Carole smiled back and knew they had done their job well. CeCe remained charming and lively in conversation, ignoring the nonverbal language passed between the two queen bees.

The site, the ambiance, and the room full of people they loved were perfect for Phoebe. Drew had planned something she would never forget. Dinner had been a humorous evening, with stories freely flowing on both sides of the family. All the attendees enjoyed the atmosphere of laughter, love, and happiness. By the end of dinner, both families were enjoying the merge of the bayou and the sea. Phoebe thought she saw tears in Richards's eyes intermittently as he glanced around the table. She felt his haunted memory of grief of souls departed but a joy to see them bloom in this gathering. Richard was full of life, and he made everyone happy who was around him. Bob also became a teary-eyed mess when he made the toast. "If Charley and Ali were here, they would be so proud." Bob had to stop for a moment to collect his emotions. "Bless the day they brought us, Michael. Drew came as such a wonderful surprise to us all. Now we share our angel, Phoebe, and our families are back together again." The dinner celebration ended early in the evening, everyone. Traveling and activities had taken their toll. While Danny led the men on a tour of the distillery, which produced the strawberry wine on the property, someone quickly took Phoebe back to her parents' home, where she slept soundly until she left for her wedding in the morning.

Far from the inn and the distillery, Myles and Ian had joined up. A recreational vehicle parked by the marina was part of the escape plan.

"Thanks for your help in preparing the gumbo for me, Myles. That was a nice touch."

"Hey, not a problem. I would do anything to make that angel happy."

“I know what you mean,” Ian said, looking out over the inter-coastal waterway.

“He’s a good guy. I see that already.” Myles just fingered the neck of the bottle. “I agree. He’s a good-looking fellow with lots of money."

"So are we!" Ian interjected.”

Myles added. “She doesn’t need a traveling troubadour or moonshiner like us with the group we hang around.”

“Your right, Myles.” Ian kept looking into the water with no expression. “It’s a shame.”

“An awful shame!” Myles added, shaking his head affirmatively.

Ian turned and shared a devilish smile with his friend. “My life is in the good shepherd’s hands, as my saintly mother always said when she had something she wasn’t supposed to keep. Now, let’s get out of here before we both cry, and Danny finds us too pitiful to drive home.”

When Drew returned to the inn with the men, he knew it had been a rouse by all the meddling family members, both male and female. He accepted the defeat of his plan and laughed it off as part of the family. At least Mr. Farmer hadn't sent him down an old road at night for an hour. Grandfather Robichaud created that little gimmick for Drew’s father to test his intentions when Michael had been courting Drew’s mother. The family’s hearts on both sides were big. That’s the way Drew wanted to be in his life.

The morning came, and the plan went off without difficulty. At 9:00 AM, two limousines arrived on one of the populated barrier islands off the coast of Georgia.

Others came in staggering waves. Drew checked off the list that Phoebe made as her essential items. On the request list was a grand piano. Uncle Jesse volunteered to play the piano as the bride had requested a song few would have heard before. Drew thought it looked perfect as the sun beamed on the water in the distance and glistened. A sailboat or two passed during the service. Rows of camellias were still in bloom in the adjoining garden. Phoebe wanted to see natural flowers, not one's cut and placed in a vase. The hotel staff completed the critical tasks. On the walk to the chapel, Drew was told that when the gate attendant stopped a limousine to ask what the purpose of the hotel was, Cid bobbed out of the back of the limo with his 6.2 frame enhanced with lean muscle and leaned against the limo.

"We are the groom's front line." The man standing guard at the gate didn't require any further verification and allowed the limo to go on without hesitation. Drew smiled when Uncle Jesse shared the story. Big Cid was the one guy Drew trusted as a brother. It was essential to have him there.

In the chapel at 10:54, the couple were speaking their vows. A few minutes later, the Chaplin announced the new husband and wife to the guests. Everyone followed to enjoy a New Orleans-style brunch. Sparkling beverages circled about the guests. A variety of French pastries and egg dishes, complete with potatoes and fruit salads, sausage, and bacon, filled the plates of the attendees. Traditional French deserts arrived for the guests after the entrée. The smells of those tables at famous restaurants in New Orleans were in the air. Friends and family enjoyed the celebration. Drew and Phoebe slipped away to have some pictures taken by a magazine that wanted to use their picture-perfect wedding for the June cover, which featured southern weddings.

Drew's manager kept the photographer safely within appropriate boundaries so that it was all done in good taste. A two-masted ketch began its way into the channel and toward the dock near the wedding party's venue as if on cue. Drew grabbed Phoebe's hand as he saw the sailing vessel and knew it was time to collect his wife and transition into the next phase of the wedding day. They slipped through the guests and inched closer to the anchoring vessel. Photos were taken. Drew waited for the signal that all was ready. Drew gently squeezed Phoebe's hand, and they were off for the last dash onto the sailboat. Phoebe threw her bouquet off the side into the arms of an unexpecting female who had arrived with Uncle Jesse. *Could he be the next to walk the plank in the Farmer's family?* It was a delightful thought

The sailboat set sail with the couple on board. Phoebe's body relaxed with the rocking movement of the craft upon the water. The ketch rolled back into the watery passageway towards the open sea and along its coast, past the watching guests and beyond the ancient maritime forest that kept sentinel along the Georgia coast.

"How was your day so far?" Drew asked once the boat was out of view of the guests.

Phoebe raised her chin to soak in the feel of the sunshine and breeze on her face. "Perfect!" She picked up a bag on the deck and opened it to find some sunscreen. She took the ointment and rubbed it on Drew's cheeks and down his neck. "There's one thing you left off my list, Drew."

Feeling the bliss of a tender touch, he opened his eyes in amazement. "What was that?" he asked with some concern.

"I loved it all," Phoebe said, nuzzling his neck. However, I put on the list that I wanted something Italian on the menu. My one day to splurge on all the carbs I wanted with the best Italian cuisine and a glass of wine," Phoebe added jokingly.

Drew smiled back. "I don't want to disappoint you."

"No, it was perfect, just the way it was."

"No, no, you wanted Italian. I didn't want to let you down. I just thought it might be better if you had your manicotti and your glass of whatever beverage you desired looking off the balcony on the Amalfi Coast so you could savor the natural flavors of local cuisine and not the vastly imitated stuff we have here.

Phoebe's eyes lit up, and her lips perked up in each corner, showing off a fresh, velvety pink color framing the most delightful expression. "We are going to Italy! Drew, is that what you are saying?" Phoebe kissed Drew from his forehead to his neck with a happy squeal. "Is that what all this has been about the last few weeks? All those vaccination records and passport shots. I thought you were planning a Mexico or Caribbean honeymoon. But we are going to the Mediterranean!"

Drew calmly said, "I have to make a business stop in France at the request of my grandfather. His old French roots are important to him as he's grown older. It's tied in with the company. I wanted to comply with his request. I hope you will understand. I will see what it all means when we get there."

"I have the most wonderful husband!"

"That's true, of course, and I have the most beautiful wife inside and out. It does not matter what she wears or doesn't wear, come to think of it. I like it all!"

"I waited to have you back with me each time you left during the season. It was so painful toward the end. I wanted it to end. I was so lonely without you. I knew you were doing what you do and were a hero. I felt so guilty for wanting to keep you to myself."

"We don't have to talk about that now. I felt very jealous while I was away, and I'm not jealous by nature. Ian, the kilt, and plaid man, was at the top of my list."

Phoebe laughed. "He is not Scottish; he is Irish."

"Well, he acts like a Scotsman around whiskey and has that thing with his voice that all the ladies love."

"Drew, Ian has lots of charm, but you're the one I chose."

"It's even worse than that. You know the Reverend Hobbs at the city church that you help once a week.

"Yes?"

"I am requesting that we cannot attend a church of the denomination when we are in Savannah. He told me at Thanksgiving when I was here that if he were only thirty years younger, he would snap you up."

"Reverend Hobbs is a good and humble man. However, he is bold and wears brown socks with his sandals most of the year because of his frequent flair-ups with gout. He preached a lot from the book of Job. Have you read that book in the Bible? It doesn't make me smile until the very end."

"Well, I was being ridiculous with that thought. The pastor did see you five times to my one in December. It made me jealous." Drew placed his nose against Phoebe's hair.

"Is that lavender?"

"It's an English peony."

"I love the fragrance. I don't care if it's English or French. It would smell heavenly in any country you wore it."

"What about you, Drew? When I'm not with you, should I be jealous? You are the quarterback of a pro team who travels the circuit where beautiful women travel."

"Yes, I think you need to be concerned. I have a strong attachment to my center and frontline, who protect me from the sweaty foul-mouth defensive lineman and tackles that want to make content with my body each weak. There is also a fondness for the big man who sends me to plays and reviews films with me on Mondays. Another enormous threat to my affection is from a steel wool textured gray-haired coordinator who pats my bottom when I run out to the field in those tight-fitting uniforms we are expected to wear. Now, I'm not sure what his actual intentions are. He has been my counselor, philosopher, teacher, and sounding board this past season, and I couldn't have done it without him. However, I also connected with a mermaid who brought magic whenever she was near. That is one dangerous female." Drew looked tenderly into Phoebe's eyes. "She used the furry pug as an irresistible bate at Christmas, and I couldn't leave her presence. She captured me, and I was a happy prisoner. I never wanted to be free again." Drew ended his conversation with a kiss. The boat continued to travel up the coastline to its destination. The occupants savored each sway of the waves.

♥

Chapter 10

Drew and Phoebe had planned to spend most of the off-season on the coast. There were trips back to north Georgia to address business with the team or other things that needed his attention. Drew and his new wife also took a trip to visit his family in Louisiana. He and Phoebe were happy to share the tales of their adventures on their honeymoon. Phoebe particularly loved the shopping in Milan and Paris. She practiced her French every place she went. Drew praised her natural way with the merchants, who spoke no English. She won them over with her warmth and genuine love for the people, especially in the small towns. With her mother-in-law's great gift of style in mind, Phoebe brought CeCe a gift of Parisian lipsticks and fragrances from a list of French women's favorites. She even chose to wear her makeup in a European style with minimal color except for a touch of bright red on her lips for her everyday look.

Drew had no complaints at all. Phoebe's little presentation of trying on all the colors that night after exploring the shops in

Paris was an enjoyable distraction to her husband. Who knew a man could enjoy a day of shopping? However, Phoebe was not a selfish woman and let Drew have his moments too. He had his time on a boat learning the lessons of navigating in the ancient waters of Greek mythology in a small cove on the southern end of Italy. Finally, he came back to the state's bronzed as a Greek God.

Rona and Richard were delighted to see the couple return from their honeymoon. Drew's grandparents enjoyed every bit of the stories of walking in Paris and seeing the lights at dusk. It reminded them of earlier days when they had walked the same streets and sat at cafes watching people. They, too, had been young once and remembered those romantic times when dancing shadows filled the wall as the moonlight sneaked in through the doors leading to the balcony. Likewise, memories kept Richard and Reba comforted as they have gotten older when their physical bodies reminded them of the precious little time that remained to share the company with loved ones.

Drew spent a good deal of time with his grandfather on this trip. They had a lot to catch up with and celebrate. Richard had recorded the last game, and they watched from the kickoff to the end. He made his colorful, narrated remarks throughout the whole playback. Thank goodness there was only the family present. In times like these, Reba was an intelligent woman. Uncle Steven attempted to bring some gentility to the play-by-play action for the ladies' sake. Drew had not seen the game on video in its entirety as he had rushed home to prepare for the wedding.

Seeing grown men running up and down the field for almost three hours was entertaining. It was more pleasant this time, as he did not feel the stabbing pain from the stubbing of his fingers when he hit the ground from the tackle in the second quarter. His wrist felt a lot better now, too. Drew didn't need the kinesthetic taping anymore for pain. Drew gave credit to Phoebe for some of that. She had that special touch when he ached all over.

Richard chimed in after a few more plays in the third quarter. "Here it comes, the old Frogman play. I didn't know it was still in the playbooks after all these years. Drew, who gave you that call?"

Drew looked at his grandfather, questioning. "I made up the play during practice the week of the game. I shared it with the coach and the squad. We played around with-it during practice. I didn't think we would use it in a game. Before entering the field after halftime, I told the coach about the play and reminded the guys. Remember the play if we got in a certain situation in the other quarter. One of the players triggered the idea while I was on the sidelines when we got back after the half. I signaled to the coach when we got into the fourth quarter, and the offense went into formation on the field. He nodded his head. After a few plays to move the ball down the field, I made the call. We did it with that play."

"Amazing! I hadn't seen it since Frogman made that play in college. He won the game for us in one of the bowls' games in his second year. The next year he injured his back on a play and never played again."

Drew looked at his grandfather with a questioning look. "You knew someone called Frogman?"

Grandfather Robichaud smiled back. "I was aware of a player named Frogman. I didn't know him personally then, as I had never played football. But that was his nickname on the team. Everybody knew him by his nickname on campus."

"Did Grandpa Howard ever play on the team?"

"I can't say, Drew. I don't remember everyone that was on the team. Some players sat on a bench a lot. Those are the guys you never heard about."

"Phoebe, did your grandfather ever play football?" Drew asked as he turned in astonishment to his wife.

"I don't know. My grandfather never talked about it. I don't ever remember him watching a Sunday game. But he did watch your games when he got to know you, and we started seeing each other. However, now that I think about it, he hasn't watched a game college or pro all the years I can remember until this year."

"Does he have a bad back?"

"He has a rod on his back. He's had it for many years. I don't know when or how he was injured. He doesn't do a lot of lifting or physical labor. He's always been a professor and a researcher. I never heard a word about his injury my entire life."

"Did you and Charley and Frogman attend the same college?" Drew asked.

"Yes, I was younger than Charley by a couple of years, and I didn't know him or Ali while they were in college. I was a harder edgy chap compared to the man you see today. The refinery provided me part-time and made substantial money working there. I thought I would invest in myself instead of wasting all my money on liquor and other entertainments," Grandfather Robichaud admitted. "Then I met Rona, the angel sent to save me from myself. Your grandmother shined and buffed me up over the years." I look rather good now. I may have been a handsome devil, but I am a mess on the inside."

"Grandfather, you are loved, and we appreciate you more than you will ever know," Drew remarked as he hugged his grandfather. "You know, Phoebe and her family are huggers, so you'll have to get used to that around us."

Grandfather Robichaud smiled with a slight blush. "I think I can get used to that stuff. Rona has been working on me with her hugs and kisses for years, too."

Rona chimed in. "CeCe. I might have to borrow one of those lipsticks from you. My influence has been working on your father."

While Drew was back with his parents for a visit, he also loaded up on his mother's cooking while he was visiting. Healthy food was good for longevity and the stamina of an elite athlete, but his mother's cooking was good for living life to the fullest with no regrets. He appreciated all the wisdom he gained from his time with his family. His batteries we recharged, and decisions awaited him in the coming weeks. He wanted to be sure he was making the right choices.

One day, after returning from Louisiana, piles of laundry were sitting on the bedroom floor. Phoebe had sorted the piles before she left for the bakery.

Drew sat at the side of the bed, rubbing his whiskers. "I guess this is my duty as a dutiful husband." He said out loud to himself. Drew sipped his coffee. He decided to take a run first. He stole the t-shirt from the dresser and proceeded to the living room, where presents still sat cluttering floor space and table surfaces. Phoebe had created a system to organize where the gifts were to be stored and who sent them. Drew didn't want to mess with the secret code, so he left everything where it was. Propped up in the entry was a box propped up against the wall addressed to Drew. It was a large package in a nondescript brown box. It didn't even have a shipping label. Drew was curious about that. He assumed someone he knew had given it to Phoebe to bring home. He could wait, but his curiosity was high this morning, and his wife must have known about it, or she wouldn't have it for him to see. *Wonder what was in the box?* It was something else that would have to wait.

The next priority in Drew's eyes was to clear his head. So, onto the pavement in his jogging outfit and sneakers, he went. Socks was in the left flanking position. The thoughts started pouring in as his toes touched the payment. Training camp was coming soon, and his contract was being negotiated. Bozeman was healthy again and didn't like the thought of facing his teammate for the quarterback position. However, Drew didn't think he could sit on the bench again after he got the taste of being a leader. Bozeman had been a class act through the entire season, including when the playoffs were underway, and he was released to come back as a starter.

The four-inch legs of his little friend gave out by the time he made it three-quarters of the way back from the marina. Drew tucked the soft ball under his arm and returned home. He noticed Uncle Jesse was at home. The man must have taken some time off. Drew thought he might stop in a little later. One mile turned into four more before Drew turned back onto the lane where he lived. It was a straight shot to the cottage and into the shower. Drew passed by the package that he had noted earlier. He could hear his phone buzzing on the kitchen table. He looked at it with narrowed eyes and felt the message wait.

Drew then dashed into the shower, hoping to decipher what was still stirring up his peace. But it was the same something he felt in California before the game. It was the same noise he'd heard for the last several months.

Phoebe balanced it all. She had her work, made time for their relationship, and found that quiet time that nobody was allowed to invade. He knew she still took her walks down by the pier while he went back to work after supper. He wondered if he should be out there with her. She never asked him to go with her in the evening. There was so much more to learn about his mermaid. Drew walked out of the bedroom. He looked at his phone but opened the box addressed to him. After a few cuts into the tape and ripping the box and filler. He found the painting he had seen in the bakery many months earlier. There was a card attached. It read.

I was your grandfather's wingman for two years before my accident. Now my precious granddaughter is yours. Keep her safe and loved in this lifetime, and I will meet you with open arms in the next. You have also proven that you've heard that voice that sets your path in a different direction than most. I believe Charley gave this to me for safekeeping. When I played football, my job was to guard and protect. When given the ball, I would fly. I did that to the best of my ability.

Frogman

Drew sat in astonishment. The tapes were left out in the loft. It was Phoebe's grandfather's response to Grandpa Howard. "Wow!" he exclaimed out loud. Drew looked again over at the driveway next door. Uncle Jesse's red truck wasn't outside now. Drew went to go over to the phone. Phoebe had texted him a couple of messages. The last just 15 minutes ago was that Phoebe's grandfather had passed away peacefully in his chair at home, so she was going to be at her mother's house. Drew changed his clothes to something more businesslike and headed across the bridge to his in-laws' home. It was a significant loss, yet as with life, there is new growth coming. Drew learned recently that people never truly go away if they have faith. Some signs let one know those who have died are still watching over those they love.

Chapter 11

AFTER EIGHT WEEKS OF marriage, Phoebe dreaded the time that Drew would start the preseason routine. He hadn't said much about it, but it was somewhat awkward not to talk about it. Some changes were inevitable. She let the lease lapse on her cottage on the oceanfront. Drew would not give up the home on Willow Way anytime soon. Her old life was packed away in boxes now. Drew spent a lot of time when he was home in the studio. Although he never minded when Phoebe came up to check on him, he seemed deeply involved in something he was working on. She knew his contract had not been agreed upon yet, which had him thinking and adjusting his plans. Drew seemed happy. So, what was going on in his head?

"Drew, I'm taking mother and grandma shopping today in Charleston. I suspect you don't want to come.

"He smiled with his pearl-white teeth over the bathroom sink and shook his head in agreement as he proceeded to lather his face.

"Love to share the day with three lovely ladies, but I have some critical duties today. First, our four-legged dependent is going to the beauty shop and shots for the first time at Dr. Braun's.

"I should be here for her first time! I was the one who caused my little one to be put in the crate last night."

"No, her curiosity got her in the crate last night. Don't worry. I got you covered. Besides, I have some team things to discuss with my agent. He is coming to town to talk with me in person today. Where would you recommend I take him?'

"It depends. Do you want to play golf too? I suggest taking him over to Ian's place for lunch after a round of golf. There are a few less formal off the main drag when you cross over the inlet. But, of course, that would be on the way back from the courses in South Carolina. Is he flying to Savannah or the airport on the island this time?

"I think he's coming into Savannah this time. I think this is business, and he is flying back out."

"If you are going to be casually dressed, I would take him to Myles's place. If he's coming in suit clothes, I would say the old mansion would be a viable choice downtown. Ian's is still a possibility, too, as it has a great lunch menu of local cuisine. The ambiance at Ian's is less touristy. The bar side has a room that looks like an English manor library. It's very conducive to power lunches.

"Great ideas! We'll see what he feels like when he arrives."

"You could always take him to the bakery and fill him with iced tea and a slice of key lime cake. Uncle Jesse's working today. I will ensure he cuts an extra large piece for both of you."

"Now that's the winner! But do you think you will have time to stop to pick up some tea while you're up there? You know my mom loves peach and green tea."

"I remember. I will make sure we find some to send to CeCe. Anything else?"

"No, just buy something that you like. I am picturing you in something we saw in Capri on our honeymoon. Anything like that would surely please me."

"Well then, I think I shall have a very nice time today thinking of how to keep my husband happy!" By 9:00, Phoebe was ready to run out the door. "Hey, babe, it's time for me to leave."

"I know, but I will miss you while you're gone. So don't rush, but text me if it looks like you're going to be after 6:00 PM. It just allows me to know that you're okay."

"Will do!"

"Bye." Drew quickly kissed her cheek before Phoebe ran out the door." An hour later, Drew finished his run and showered. Socks, the pug, was then carried off to the vet. Hopefully, she learned the pup learned a lesson this time that Phoebe's lipstick was not met for her. However, the vet said he could make her fur white again, so Drew's mission today was to drop Socks off and get her shampooed along with some shots.

Marcus Bass, Drew's agent, called at about 11:00 from the airport. He was open to any place to meet but thought a private area would work best. Drew accepted Phoebe's' plan and gave him the bakery's address. They could use the private room. Drew texted Uncle Jesse, and the plan was in motion.

Thirty minutes had gone by, and Drew's face had changed from a warm greeting to a stoic expression as he sat across the table from Marcus. "I wanted you to hear the options from me in person, Drew; before it gets leaked in the news. You do have a choice. It may not feel like that right now. Everybody seems interested, but what's best for Drew may not be the one on the table. Your team wants you, but they can't afford two rock-star quarterbacks. Having Bozeman back makes the owners cringe at boosting your contract up with his, but they also know who took them to the show. They haven't made a contract offer, but I'm sensing it's not going to be where it should be after last year's performance, and they know it. It also means you would be Bozeman's backup again. That doesn't seem fair, but he's the one with the hefty contract being the experienced quarterback in the middle of his 3-year warranty. There is another team that has been stirring the pot a little. It's in the northeast. My feeling is that they will pay what you deserve. Phoebe made a big impression during the season when she met with some of the folks in the boxes.

Drew's eyes went from hazel to steel. "That deal won't happen. I would never take

Phoebe there, and where I go, Phoebe goes."

"I am hearing the potential for a big package."

"The answer is no! I will not participate in any further discussion on the matter. It's not the money, and it's not the organization." "Drew, I don't want you to destroy your career like this. Some go out because of injury. Others bring their unpleasant habits to the game. You're the perfect player with a story that makes headlines. You finely are getting the opportunity to play. Live anywhere you want, just go there and play! The network people think you and Phoebe are a perfect couple. The public relations people are drooling at the mouth up there to have both of you. They think you and Phoebe would make great spokespeople for the organization and foundations they support."

Drew instantly turned into a blazing fire beneath his intense, controlled fury. "Marcus, the time has come to end our business relationship. I will have my attorney send you a legal document ending your representation agreement. I will allow my attorney to determine the correct date for the end of the agreement based on the original terms, but it ends today. If you respect our former friendship, don't ever bring this discussion up again or approach my wife in any way."

"Drew, what did I say to bring this reaction? It will be out in media outlets today!"

Drew got up from his chair. "I'm sorry to go, but I need to take care of some business. Have a safe trip back." He then steered Marcus out of the building. Drew met with Uncle Jesse for a few minutes before leaving himself. He pulled out of the lot and drove a couple of blocks down the street to a church parking lot. He tried calling Phoebe, but there was no answer.

Drew texted her a message. A security guard was starting around the building, but another gentleman in the adjoining annex came out to intervene. Drew paid little attention.to either figure. His own emotions captured him. I gave it all, and this is where it led me. Should I stay caged, filling the bench for many more years before they spit me out like old chewing gum? The second idea wasn't an option at all.

Just then, Drew's phone blew up. He answered it calmly. "Hey, sweetheart. Are you enjoying yourself?"

"You know we are." Phoebe giggled. "I don't need anything. That's my problem. I'll tell you what we did when I get back. We decided to cut the day short. I'll be home to make dinner. Any suggestions?"

"No peanut butter and jelly are fine with me if I can...Oh man, I forgot to pick up Socks! Let me go so I can bring her home! I'll see you when you get back."

"Okay. I love you!"

Drew couldn't say anything while Phoebe was still out with her family. He just hoped they kept her occupied enough that she didn't hear anything until he could talk with her. After a call to his attorney's office, he was ready to turn the key. A figure came walking toward his vehicle, and this one he recognized.

"Drew, what's up?"

"Danny, I'm just about to go get Socks.

Where did you come from?"

"I drove past the front street and saw your car with you. It seemed odd, so I thought I would check in on you. What's up?'

“Nothing, nothing I want to talk about,” Drew said.

“You wouldn’t be in an empty parking lot unless there’s an issue. It looks like you need an ear to hear what’s on your mind.”

Drew had a discouraging look and didn’t want to make eye contact with Danny to show what a burden he was carrying just then. Finally, drew spoke, “Something is going entirely wrong, and I don’t know what to do about it?”

“Well, that sounds ominous.”

“Maybe, I just need to think.” Drew replied.

“Could it be about staying with the team?” Danny asked.

“Maybe. Why do you ask?” Drew looked up, wondering how Danny hit the bull’s eye.

“I heard something commented on one of the stations in the last hour.”

“Well, I guess what I heard today was right. I’m trying to figure out what it all means. What did the host say?” Drew looked up at Danny. .

Danny looked indifferent but responded. “These two sports reporters indicated that the team might be negotiating a different kind of contract than you might have expected coming off a winning season. The coaching staff is going back to put Bozeman back as Q1. That may not leave much room for a salary hike for the quarterback that brought them their dinner plate last year.”

“It’s just all business,” Drew responded rather stoically.

"I could see how that puts a bad taste in your mouth. It makes you want to spit some tobacco out on the dirt and stomp on it, doesn't it."

Drew got the image and had to agree.

"Does Phoebe know yet?" Danny asked.

"I don't think so unless she has heard something today. She is out with your mother and Carole today. I hope they have kept her busy until I can talk with her."

"There's a high chance of that. They mentioned another team that had an interest in you in the news broadcast. They indicated you'd be a perfect fit," Danny added.

"I'm not going there. I can promise you," Drew responded.

"I believe you. There may be an option that opens. You are at the end of your contract, I understand."

"Yes, that's true." Drew presented an outward expression of a flat affect, not to show the emotional upheaval he was feeling. "That's what I need to think about right now."

"I hear you." Danny paused for a moment and then added his sage advice. "Phoebe and I grew up in a home where we were taught to listen carefully when something lifechanging was happening around us. That's been one of the wisest things our parents taught us from when we were young. That is how we get our directions in life and business. We learned to listen to the quiet within the storm to help us know what to do next."

"Thanks, Danny. I know you mean well. I'm trying hard to listen. I guess I was taken a bit by surprise today. It's all going to work out. You know I'm feeling more at peace about it already.

Let me go pick up Socks at the vet. I only wanted to leave her for a couple of hours. I know that four-legged puppy will be eager to run off some energy, and that's what I feel I need to do right now."

"That sounds like a good plan. I'll be around this evening if you want to talk."

"Thank you, Danny."

There was a lightness in Drew's emotions as he left the parking lot. He pushed the peddle and traveled down the narrow city blocks reaching the bypass that took him back to the island. *There will be instructions if there is a fork in the road ahead. I just had to listen and be willing to follow.*

Drew picked up Socks and rewarded her with a burger with no bun, cheese, or condiments from a hamburger place close to the house. When the woman at the window smiled back at Drew and complimented the precious face, Drew was ready to wink back for fun until he realized she was talking about the pup. Finally, Drew acknowledged that he was having a terrible day when his puppy got more sugar today than his owner. He headed home without any more stops. Once he arrived home, he made a couple of calls. He also listened to a couple more while packing an overnight back. Phoebe hadn't returned home yet and was concerned about that, but he would phone her if she hadn't reached home by 4:30 PM. He wasn't sure what he was going to say anyway. When the alarm on his clock went off, Drew grabbed his things and put them by the door. He put Socks in the sunroom with her play toys, fresh water, and some snacks. Phoebe would be home soon. When the limousine drove up to the drive, Drew quickly gathered his things and left a note for Phoebe on the counter. An attempt was later made with a text before Drew reached the airport. Of course, it wasn't quite the same, but there was some consolation: she would feel his pillow when she went to sleep and remember the sweet words from this morning before he left.

"Antoine, let's head out. You know where we are going," said Drew.

"Yes, Mr. Taylor."

A few minutes into the drive, Drew began to call Phoebe on her phone.

Phone picked up and said, "Drew, I'm almost home. I just dropped off everybody."

"Sweetheart, I am on my way to meet Steven and my grandfather, who is in Savannah today. I haven't seen them yet, but I have talked with them. I am flying back with them to Louisiana on a charter flight. I'm planning to be back tomorrow evening."

"Drew, something is happening, isn't it?"

"I think so, I'm not sure enough even to talk with you about it, but I will as soon as I can put my arms around it all. And what it means for us. You are part of the discussion, and you will have a say, but I think I need to deal with this sign being in front of me. Then I can take another step with your input. Your brother told me today that your family faces things by listening and waiting for directions. That's what I'm doing right now, sweetheart. I hate leaving you there tonight without seeing you before I left. I'm trying to make the right choice here. I want you to trust me."

"Okay. Drew, this is a big something, isn't it?" Phoebe asked.

"I think so. I wasn't expecting any of this today. Although my life is typically predictable, ever since I met the violet-eyed mermaid behind the basket of muffins, my life has taken on an adventure I would have never dreamed of living. I love sailing the waves with you beside me. We are near our destination. Phoebe. I'll see you tomorrow night."

"Okay, tell your family I'm sending my love!" Phoebe said with concern in her voice.

"I will. I promise. Goodbye, Phoebe." Drew's phone went silent.

Phoebe dropped the phone on the sofa. She looked around at the things that she loved. *They're just things. I never truly owned anything I had in this world. Forever isn't defined by my dictionary but by God's. I promised I would follow God's plan which was not my own, no matter how good my plan was. I knew I would not receive all I wanted in this life.*

Phoebe looked at Socks. "I guess you were preparing my heart against my self-indulgence, my friend." Socks came over to Phoebe and whimpered at her feet, making an endearing request. Phoebe obliged by picking Socks up and tickling her behind her ears. "I was so mad at you for ruining my favorite French lipstick last night. I had grand prideful plans of wearing it on a special evening with my favorite black dress on the arm of my handsome husband as we mingled with important people." She looked down and smiled. "I am happy we got you cleaned up today. Red does not look good on you, my friend, when it's on your paws and whiskers. Phoebe put Socks back on the floor. "You did me a favor, Socks, but please don't dabble with the fuchsia-colored one. It would be so much harder to replace." Phoebe looked down at the blonde fur ball and led it to the kitchen door to allow Socks time outside as she sat on the patio watching the puppy frolic about in the yard. She heard a classical piano piece of music coming from next door. Uncle Jesse must be practicing for his Wednesday night performance. Burying his knuckles in three-inch sticky bun dough at 6:00 AM, Jesse amazingly stretches them delicately over ivory keys making beautiful music when he is away from the bakery and work.

In the skies above Birmingham, Drew Taylor was finding out about a new set of plays. Had this been what he had been preparing for all his life? Less than twenty-four hours ago, the convertible-driving quarterback with his pooch sat at an outdoor picnic table at a roadside pull-out overlooking the marsh and pondered his career options. There, another voice had reached out to him as he sat watching the egrets land in the trees on the small island that appeared at low tide when the peaks of the waves rolled away.

"Steven and I are here in Pooler. We want you to come back with us today. Will you come?" Richard's voice was the calming balm that Drew heard over the fog in his head. Before the midnight hour, he would be in Louisiana.

The next few days were a whirlwind. Drew returned to Savannah by supper the following day, just as he promised Phoebe.

Uncle Jesse had watched the limousine turn onto Willow Way, wiped his brow, and went back to mowing the lawn. *It is becoming a trend around here.* He laughed and kept steering the riding lawn mower around the crepe myrtle in the front yard. Drew decided to be honest and talk with Phoebe about the latest events. Finding the leash, he took Socks for a walk with Phoebe beside him. They walked down by the marina and out to the pier. Then, they extended their trek to the side streets of the neighborhood. There was a comforting feeling walking within the tunnel created by the gray-colored Spanish moss draping the branch of tree limbs shading the lane and the sidewalk. The sun peeped through the gaps warming the faces of those who strolled beneath this lush passageway.

"I'm sorry I had to leave without telling you goodbye," Drew started. "Something came up yesterday morning, and I needed to address it."

"I knew something must have happened. So, I called Danny, and he didn't say much. Danny says a lot when he feels something needs to be said, but he didn't tell me anything except he saw you."

"Phoebe, I'm not going back to play with the team?"

"Any team or just the team you've been playing for this past year?"

"I'm not going back to football, Phoebe?"

"Okay. It sounds like you've made a decision." Phoebe responded. She squeezed his hand a little tighter. "I'm okay with that." Phoebe attempted to listen with her heart. She knew Drew had struggled with something the day he left for Louisiana. Was there something else he had been working with that she had not seen?

"Thank you. I know this is going to sound crazy. My grandfather thought it was wise to immerse ourselves in France for about a year if I took on this new role. The company bought a small facility in France to strengthen the international leg of my grandfather's company. We are to show goodwill to the current management and their families as part of the merger." Drew attempted to lighten the moment. "We do both speak French." Drew looked at Phoebe with raised eyebrows, indicating that he was seeking her excitement with this option.

Phoebe's facial expression changed immediately to excitement as she processed his words. "Wait! I am slowly processing everything. Did I just hear you say something about France? That's where Paris is located? What is this about my husband?" Phoebe looked up at her husband, searching his face for the meaning of this conversation.

"It's all technical, but my father was to rise as an executive within my grandfather's company before he died. My grandfather remained at the helm with Steven as second in command. Steven was aware of my grandfather's plans. Steven and my grandfather are both getting older now. My grandfather had hinted about some things during our conversation at Christmas. Then, again when I was in California preparing for the big game out there. When my grandfather called me yesterday telling me he was here in town with Steven, I knew why. I also had some troubling news early in the day about the team and the prospects of where I may be playing football next year. I know what it means now to have this conviction inside of me. Although my family didn't force me to make this decision, I decided this was what I was led to do, not by my family or the team. There's a power at work here, Phoebe, and I can't ignore the voice in my head or my heart. But, Phoebe, it also impacts you, and I don't want to hurt us and our life together."

"I go where you go, Drew. If it's France, we go to France," Phoebe said and gave Drew a reassuring smile.

"Sweetheart, I will buy one of those French lipsticks in every color at that store we shopped at during our honeymoon if it keeps that smile on your face."

"I can see some benefits of this move already." Phoebe took her hands and placed them on his chest. "If this is the right choice for you. I will follow." She paused as if she was trying to hear his true heart." How much time do we have?"

"I think my grandfather was thinking of 30 days. My contract runs out officially

Friday. I haven't notified the team of my official retirement plans. I can do that today. I want to list the property in the mountains immediately. I'm not planning on selling this place. I might put a caretaker to watch over the property for a year. I'm unsure what to do with it, but I won't sell it. We can get some help from our contacts in France to line up an apartment. We can find a rental cottage by the sea if you like. I will gather more information about where we would need to be and send the information to an agency that handles rental properties in the area. They can be our arm over there while we are making the transition. I will let you communicate with them as I trust you to decide what we might need to call someplace home for a year."

Phoebe looked squarely into Drew's eyes. "I have confidence in all that you do and will do. "We'll be fine. I think I will like this, Drew, even though I am terrified of this adventure. I will put love in your coffee each morning and buy fresh baguettes from the market to make your peanut butter and jelly sandwiches when you come home. If I am with you, I will make a home where we are happy."

"I have faith in you too, Phoebe. You will shine wherever we are on this planet. That sounds like we need to get this plan in place quickly. Let's request from our contact in France that our home has a balcony that faces the ocean or the vineyard as I want to catch your silhouette dancing on the terrace through the French doors against the backdrop of the sunset or moonlight.

Chapter 12

It had been a year since Drew and Phoebe had left to live in Savannah and relocated near Paris, the city of charm and French culture. Drew and Phoebe did this at a request by the family patriarch. His advice to them when he sent them off to France as the company's representative was to learn to appreciate the people. It amazed Drew sometimes as he learned more about his grandfather's dealings. Although the choices may have looked like financial maneuvering, there was also a soul to how his grandfather had built his business. The couple found that they grew so much together. The couple's French became more fluent and used it as their language of choice when they were out in public. Bike and scooter riding in the countryside became a weekend adventure. Drew and Phoebe worked on building relationships in a country not of their upbringing. It was like being naked in a fishbowl. People would come and meet them just to observe how strange or different they may do something. Some greeted the differences with laughter and entertainment. Others disliked how they did things and were happy to express their dislike with sarcasm or belittlement. Drew and Phoebe shared those times when the homesickness outweighed the purpose and their quest to do their best. They were diligent about respecting the differences but not giving away who they were in the areas of their heart that mattered most.

In March of the following year on their arrival, another wind began to blow. The couple answered the call to come home to the states. Steven had passed away with few knowing the severity of his illness with the company. Drew believed a select few knew the secret before Drew had left for France. Drew had accepted his destiny. Twelve months earlier, he turned his back on what he had prepared for all his life as an athlete. Instead, twelve months had turned him into an international business executive. Returning to the United States, he would gather the rains of something he hadn't planned on being. His grandfather had put in Drew's hands the family business. Drew somberly shivered at the responsibility of it all as he departed the plane with Phoebe in New Orleans. He was facing the fact he carried the role meant for his father, who did not live long enough to fulfill his destiny. When Drew met Phoebe in the car before pulling out at the airport, he looked at his wife and tried to explain his feelings without words. "I feel my father, Phoebe. I feel like he is here with us, and he is helping me know him intimately with each choice I make. I'm scared, Phoebe. I'm not sure I can be him."

Phoebe took his hand. "Drew, he doesn't want you to imitate him. He would want you to be yourself, and you will know him intimately. Just like you learned to love the mermaid with the flour on her nose and her hair pulled back, you'll find yourself along the way."

"Phoebe, without you, I would still be on that bench waiting but never expecting to play in the big show. So instead, I prepared for nothing to change, and when it didn't, I would go home and relive the next day."

The funeral services had passed, and support was given to Maggie, Steven's wife, who would always be a part of the family. They would help her go through this period as fast or slowly as she needed. With no children to fuss over, Maggie, Steven's widow, showed great strength in pulling herself up and maneuvering through her life choices. She had never wanted to be a part of the business and kept her interest in the healing arts. That is where Maggie wished to stay. She had her practice that she would return to and fill her heart again with the compassion that was her gift. Steven had benefited from that gift all the years they had known one another. Now there would be more time to spend in that area and reach out to a larger sphere of people. Drew has some ideas. Time would tell if Maggie's wanted to take that path.

The next several weeks were a blur. Drew's new role at the top of the company's leadership would bring him back to the states. The European merger with a small company based in France was stable and easily placed in solid management. Drew was considering the plan of moving the headquarters to Savannah, which had been present since before he was born. Of course, there were other factors in that decision, but the possibility looked promising. It would be no surprise to anyone in the company to understand Drew's history, but few knew the family background, the truth never found on paper. Phoebe's roots grew deep in Savannah, and all assumed she influenced Drew's decision.

Phoebe had been quiet on the choice. All she asked for was a place that Drew and she could call home.

Chapter 13

PHOEBE WAS BURSTING WITH joy to share her secret with Drew. Finally, what she suspected before he left for a business trip to California was confirmed while he was gone. She made him promise he would take her somewhere for an entire day when he returned so she could refuel her empty tank, needing togetherness time. When Phoebe saw the exit signs for the barrier islands off the coast while Drew kept driving further south on the interstate, her face lit up.

A few hours later, Drew and Phoebe were off on another Island, only reached via a ferry or private boat. They had spent most of the late morning and afternoon walking the island's paths. They visited the old ruins, and occasionally someone would come alongside and chat for a few moments before moving on down the path to their destination. Eventually, they found a place to rest. It was a quiet nook that had some shade away from the t the pier.

"Drew, I like this place!"

"Yeah, so do I when I'm with you."

"I like seeing the horses meander on the grass. There is something peaceful about hearing they hear the clip-clop on the dirt path. I want to bring this little one here so our child can appreciate the islands' natural beauty and the sea."

Drew looked at Phoebe. "Wait just a minute. Are you saying what I think you're saying?" Drew had a look of total surprise. Phoebe didn't say another word. Instead, she raised her chin and nodded affirmatively with a big smile. Drew gave Phoebe a lengthy kiss. He took her hand. "Don't be ugly. I haven't known long. I waited until I knew for sure and then wanted to tell you in person."

"Your forgiven." Drew paused, wanting to confess his own. "When we were in France, I sabotaged where you put your pill box. I would push your stuff behind the band-aid box and kinesthetic tape. I was hoping you'd forget some things.

"You bad man, Drew! You never told me that!"

"I'm sorry. I should have trusted you more with how I felt. I have my faults." Drew tried to lift the spirit of the conversation back to a welcomed joy. "How long have you known about this bun, sweety?"

Phoebe touched her abdomen as she spoke of the family addition."

"I'm only about ten weeks along." Phoebe paused. "Drew, I want to tell our children about the day I saw your grandparents walking and laughing on the beach from my porch at the old beach house when I first moved in after leaving Maine."

Drew hugged her a little tighter but gently to avoid hurting her or the child she was carrying. "Ahh, I accepted your story as truth. However, the next generation may be skeptical. At that time, Charley had already passed by the time you moved back."

"They will understand when it happens to them one day. I will share the part about how Ali painted the picture of her and Charley while on this same island as college students during Christmas break. They'll hear that it was Charley's anniversary present from Ali. I love their story, Drew. I love your father based on all that I know of him.

"As I confessed earlier, I've got some flaws that are not always coverable."

"Well. I knew that when I said yes. I accepted my fate. You do want me to go on, don't you?"o

"I'm not sure, but yes, go on!"

"I want to tell them about the part about how my grandfather received the painting from Ali sometime after Charley died. She knew it had been Frogman that kept Charley from losing his faith when he lost your father. Quiet an important part of the story." Phoebe looked up at Drew and sought out his eyes. "Our children will learn I'm on your wing just like a wingman.

"They were people just like us trying to find their way. But, you know, Phoebe, you didn't add anything about a mermaid in this story.

"Yes, I did!"

"When did you say anything about a mermaid?" Drew tried to follow.

"I told you I saw Ali and Charley walking and laughing on the beach. That's true!"

"I have told you that I don't doubt that you thought you saw someone who looked like Ali and Charley on the beach that day."

"I'm going to tell you my side of the story again as you seemed to have forgotten some parts," Phoebe said teasingly.

Drew laughed and put a kiss on her forehead. "I do have a short memory for some things."

"I returned from Maine with my injuries. I couldn't move very well and was bandaged tightly for a while. I would pull up a sleeping bag over my lower extremities, prop my legs on a chair, and sit on the balcony facing the ocean. I mostly sat and felt sorry for myself during the first few months. That was true even after my leg had healed. I would sit on that porch for hours, looking out and listening to the tide's roar. Even when it rained, I would prop myself up and watch the storm on the horizon. Nobody could say anything that pulled me out of the slump. After the night you heard about when Ian stopped me from doing something stupid, I turned from that world of darkness. The following day, I came out, stood on the porch sipping my coffee, and talked it out with God. I wanted something to hope for again. I lost my dancing, and now my body was marked with an ugly reminder of something I never wanted to remember. I was honest with myself. What would I fill my heart with if I let go of self-pity? I looked out and saw what I believed was Ali and Charley like they were in the painting. It gave me a vision that God could provide me with something that would bring joy back into my life. Ian had been pounding in my noggin the night before as he waited for Danny to take me home from Myles's place. My mother and grandparents allowed me to hang the painting in the bakery. That's how the Burning Bush Bakery got its name.

"Lovely." Drew looked down at Phoebe and thought she looked more beautiful than ever.

"What are you talking about, Drew."

Drew sensed she knew, so he sent her a pass from a different angle. "I was thinking of a conversation with your Uncle Jesse about a similar event regarding Charley Ali and your grandparents. His rendition is a bit more colorful and has a background in the late sixties and early seventies. I knew you hadn't been born yet, so I stored it in my memory. Rock Muffin added his guitar licks to add some mood to the storytelling."

"Promise me you'll never share Uncle Jesse's version outside the two of us, okay?" Phoebe smiled.

"I promise if you never share that I prefer the strawberry wine your family produces over the imported scotch your grandfather drank. "

Drew pushed a tangle of tresses away from Phoebe's eyes that the sea breeze had sent across the shore.

"I remember my grandmother telling me the stars were like glowing candles when she and Charley came here as college students. The sounds of the island at night were like a symphony. I do believe her, but she did grow up in that sixties experience like your uncle. Do you think Charley and Ali were, you know?"

"I don't want to think what you're thinking."

"What?" Phoebe started to giggle.

"You know, flower and peace children!"

"Oh gosh! Phoebe laughed harder.

Drew lightly patted her midsection as he felt her insides roll with movement. This baby has some genes that maybe best forgotten."

"Did you find any bell-bottom pants in your grandparents' things? Maybe a tie-dyed t-shirt. It could be that they liked rock more than the crowd that listened to the crooners wearing white shoes with laces. Phoebe looked up at Drew innocently. My grandmother let me play in her closet and pick out an outfit for the sixties' dress-up day at school. I think I found a box saved from her mother."

"I didn't find anything like that. I didn't see any photos with Charley having long hair or peace symbols." Drew responded dryly.

"We did have a picture of my grandfather's college football team. I bet we would find Charley in that photo."

"I bet you are right." Drew looked at the scenery around him and understood now why some hear the calling of the sea and need to return.

"You know it is time for us to get back to the pier. I'm not as brave as Ali and Charley were with staying alone all night on the island.

"Me either!" Drew said.

"I don't think they were alone with all the wildlife around here. But, at least tonight, we won't have that around us." Phoebe said.

"I'm not sure I can promise you that," Drew led Phoebe to the path to the pier. He had hoped she hadn't caught the last kernel of truth. "Oh, look, just in time for the ferry. I can see it crossing over from the mainland now." He was happy that the news distracted Phoebe from his last remark.

The ferry brought them safely back to shore. The couple was soon traveling down the highway to the next destination for the evening. Drew, you never said where we were going tonight. Just bring a bag.

"We are going to meet up with some friends who live in the area. They've made all the arrangements."

"Do I know them?"

"Yes, you do. Cid and his wife, Rochelle, are meeting up with us."

"Oh wow! I can't wait to see them!"

"Cid and I were good friends. I'm going to warn you. I don't know what they have planned. I just told him you and I were taking the weekend off and where we would be. He took it from there. My instructions are that we are to meet up with them off the next exit. They were going to take it from there."

An hour later, Drew drove up to their lodging for the night. Cid and Rochelle parked their four-wheel drive on the side of two camping trailers. Both with a view of the ocean in front.

"Sorry about the Dust, Drew. I should have known you'd bring the convertible."

"Drew looked at his car. Dust and bugs covered the hood. He broke down laughing. "Only for you, Cid. I only continued for you, buddy!" However, the top went up as I didn't want Phoebe to have to dodge the winged carnivores while she was in the passenger seat.

"If you take it around the house tomorrow. I'll get some help to detail it. Then, I can get that thing looking shiny and sleek

just like you like it."

"Oh no! That will be part of the adventure of finding the missing pieces from this Italian model that fell off inside the car and counting the variety of flying species that can splatter down"

Rochelle and Phoebe began to tear up with laughter. They hugged each other as sisters long parted.

Cid said with a smile. "You are partially right. I think it has a history of being marshier here. The inlet is moving further south with time due to natural factors. Development to the north may be a factor too. It's a tricky balance to respect what people want and what's good for the environment. Man may win in the short run, but nature can take it back with one episode of fury. I choose to respect nature as it's mightier than me."

"I worked with many professionals to develop a plan for erosion prevention, a site for wildlife, and other issues related to concerns of man and nature in the low country. It's my passion away from football."

"Wow, I'm impressed! So, what is the deal with the campers here."

"We have an overall plan. We don't want to build on this area. Rochelle and I are building a dream home on the acreage but in a more suitable spot away from the oceanfront. Storms and ecosystems are too difficult to manage right on the beach. My parents gave us their camper. They hardly used it. I bought one similar based on theirs before we were given their trailer. I could have sold one, but I have been putting them both to use. Call it boring, but we enjoy camping out. Rochelle and I both love entertaining, so we've found different ways to enjoy what we have. A beautiful ocean view with friends is one of our favorite things to do. I brought you in a back way for fun. We are not as far away from civilization as you would think."

"Cid. I am speechless. This is incredible!" "Let me show you what we have here. You've got that trailer for the night. Rochelle and I will be getting supper ready. We have this special netting that we put around like a tent. It's great stuff and keeps away insects. We pack in and out here, so we've got this to an art. So, you come on out when you're ready.

"Okay," Phoebe said. "I'm going to accept the opportunity of freshening up and going inside. Drew can figure out all fancy the equipment and gizmos."

Drew responded, "I like that plan too. Cid shows me what I need to do. I'm a novice at this kind of thing, so I will follow your instructions."

"Let's start with the monitors. But, first, you want to make sure of the surroundings."

An hour later, Phoebe and Drew had changed. With some resistance, Phoebe put on her short cut-off shorts, the one piece of clean clothing. She packed them only for when they were in for the night after showering, which she expected would be in a hotel room at a resort. Nothing else had seemed appropriate for this evening.

Drew walked by, kissed her on the cheek, and grabbed her hand. "We're around friends, Phoebe. That's what you focus on, okay."

A couple of hours later, talking was still boisterous around the lanterns and lounge chairs in the netting between the two campers. Describing the year in France was a delightful diversion for Phoebe. Drew and Phoebe felt very relaxed and at home with their friends from Drew's football years.

Cid talked a lot on a variety of subjects. Rochelle frequently had to put in with her side of the story, which was quite different and humorous. "What the team didn't have this past year was you, man! Bozeman was a good quarterback this past season. The magic was gone. That's all I'm saying," Cid remarked.

"I get the business part of the game. However, each person needs to listen and watch for the signs when it's time to move on. I made a choice that gave me peace. Phoebe and I are happy. We were fortunate to have options that worked for us."

Phoebe grabbed his hand between the two lounge chairs. "I am delighted with Drew's choice. We were just married, and it was tough even to build a relationship when he was playing in the league!"

"Cid and I have talked about the same thing. It's tough to be without this big guy when the dog is chewing up everything in sight, and you want somebody around to say

I appreciate you."

Cid responded. "I am a big lug and forget to say those mushy words but love my prettier half, and I miss her when I'm not with her." Cid smiled back at Rochelle. Cid took another swig from his can of soda. "I've got something to show you."

As if Rochelle was reading her husband's mind, she hit Cid in the leg as a reflex action. She looked at the big linebacker with a glaring look.

Cid ignored her response for a moment. Cid nonchalantly continued. "I've got one too."

Drew's radar went on alert.

"Let me show you something." Cid got up and dropped his pants down, revealing his boxer shorts.

Rochelle blurted out, "Don't you dare, Cid!"

"No. I think Phoebe needs to see this."

Rochelle and Drew were speechless, holding back laughter. "Yes, my wife bought these for me on sale at one of the discount stores on vacation one year. It's all she could find in my size, okay!"

Drew had to laugh rather than go on the attack. Cid was trying to make a point. Seeing Cid in his underwear with a fierce four-legged cartoon character was too much for Drew to hold back his laughter.

Rochelle nodded her head affirmatively. "I learned Cid liked to stay up late on Friday nights and snuggle watching his favorite cartoon. When I saw those briefs, I couldn't resist the temptation."

"That you Rochelle. I love it when you think of me no matter what time, no matter how… or something like that. I digress for a moment, but I like them. This ugly thing I have on this left leg happened my first year in the pros. It almost cost me my potential to make it in the pros. I won't give you the details, except to say I had been a victim of some guy's anger because I was talking with an old girlfriend at a pizza joint near where I was staying that summer. Should I have been somewhere else, right? What's wrong with pizza, except for all those carbs and fats late at night? Could I have been somewhere else? Yes, I could have been. Did I have to talk with that young lady? Of course, not. I wasn't even hitting on her. I was just making small talk. The meaning behind my showing you my skivvies here is that I won't let this keep me from doing my purpose and becoming the person God says I am. Dad used to call them skivvy when he ran around the house at home.

Rochelle shook her head in her hand. Our friends aren't the same thing."

"What? My mother raised five boys!" He looked at Rochelle. "Somebody was always in underwear at my house. My mom didn't have time to fold and put away our clean clothes every day. We got used to hanging around like this."

"Oh, Cid, I need to help you mend your ways. Laundry is done as a group effort in our house."

"Yes, love. I am committed to doing my part as part of our marriage vows. So let me pull my drawers up as my point was made."

Phoebe sat in silence but had a smile on her face. She felt the warmth in Cid's merriment. Cid continued. "The person you married never once let me feel sorry for myself. He never once forgot I was there, either. I love all the guys. Drew never let me forget I was part of the team. Even when I was healing and rehabilitating and unsure, I could get this leg back up to par, Drew called or stopped to check in to visit. He even sent me 32 cases of those bags of my favorite candy on my thirty-second birthday. The delivery truck had to stack them up in my driveway. We couldn't get the car out of the garage until my brother and his friends came to help me move. Removing necrotic tissue was a nightmare each time, not because of pain. My anger stemmed from the grief of losing something like a perfectly healthy leg. After that night, it would never be the same. Something more was removed each time I went to the wound specialist." Cid looked a little sheepish. "I just wanted to say. I love your legs.

Before this guy gives me a broken one to match this one, I just want to say. I don't hide or cover up my beautiful self because I'm not perfect. You are perfect, or that guy wouldn't have selected you from all the other butterflies flying around him."

"I'm going to give you a big hug, Cid!" Phoebe said. She got up and wrapped her arms around the enormous trunk of the guy.

Drew responded. "Me too! Just beware you big lug. If you start looking at Phoebe's beautiful legs in a non-brotherly way, I will tell them about your coyote "skivvies" back in the locker room!"

"You got me there, Drew. I was thinking about someone you may want to contact if that leg gives Phoebe any problems with dancing. Leo, back with the team, might be able to help. He's the athletic trainer. He might need a doctor's supervision, but he got my movement back after my injury. I couldn't have done it without him. He works with athletes, but he may know someone

who works with dancers."

"Thank you, Cid. Maybe there is another type of therapeutic intervention. Drew, can we see about it when we get back?"

"Absolutely!"

The other thing I should say is that I'm confessing all my sins tonight. Sam's been asking about you, Drew."

"He can call me any time he wants. There are no hard feelings. I'm back in the states again. Maybe we can get together."

"He'd like that," Cid said. "Well, you bunch of party animals, I don't know about you, but I'm going to call it a night. If you want to experience a special treat, get up early. Sunrise is about 6:22 AM. Cid got up to stretch his legs.

Roxie followed his cue. "That sounds like a great idea!"

"We'll close the shades, and you stay up if you like. You may not need privacy, but we do. Cid winked back at

Phoebe as he grabbed Rochelle's hand."

"Cid, why do you toy with fire, my love."

"Because I'm married to a blazing beauty, and I love every minute!

Drew and Phoebe retired shortly as well. Tomorrow they would be back home in Savannah, planning on the workday to follow. This weekend filled Phoebe's needs which would help ward off the loneliness when Drew was away working. For some couples, the desire for togetherness waned after the first few years of marriage. Phoebe hadn't gotten to that period in their life yet and prayed it would never come."

Sometime later, Drew flopped around on the mattress, attempting to find comfort for his lengthy torso on the camper's cushions. "I don't know how Cid does it. He must have found a jumbo-size mattress he used in his camper. I am dangly over the sides everywhere."

"I could give you some room by sleeping in the space that folds down over there."

"Oh no! You stay right there. I am not going to mess up a perfect night. I will make this work." He squeezed in a little tighter and pressed his nose in her hair. Surrounded by the lavender fields they saw in France was his last thought.

The following day both couples were up and ready by daybreak. Cid brought an extra set of binoculars. "Here, take these and follow me quietly to that knoll." The group followed Cid as he walked on the sandy path that led to a high bluff closer to the sea. "Yep, they're out there!" Cid whispered to the group. Cid gave his wife his binoculars to allow her to look at the natural migration.

Drew looked as well, focusing his view on the beach. "Wow! How crazy is that!"

Phoebe moved in closer wanting to see what everyone else had seen. "What is it?"

"Here, Phoebe," Drew said. "Look right over there."

Phoebe followed the instructions. She raised the binoculars to her eyes and allowed

Drew turned her in the best direction to see what he wanted Phoebe to see.

"Loggerheads! They're moving off the beach into the water! I can see they're coming out of the holes in the dunes. How precious is that? One, two, three, four, five. They keep coming out of the hole. This is

terrific to see!"

Cid responded, "Epic! This month is the time that they mate and return. It's typical for Florida along the dunes. There hasn't been a lot of activity here in years past. I don't know if we found a wayward group or if the things, we have done to recreate the shoreline and the dunes helped bring them back to where they once lived. All the neighbors who have homes in this cove have been respectful of the sound and special lighting on the structures built around the water line. That's one of the reasons it would appear there is no one for miles. There are people around, but we try to respect the nature around us."

"Cid and Rochelle, thank you. I can't believe we were here when this was happening." Phoebe said.

"Phoebe said it for me. The turtle migration was the icing on the cake. But, man, I want to say I am so glad to see you again, my big brother!" Drew said.

"Ahh, it's mutual, Drew. Speaking of brothers, you need to start the poker game back up, especially in the early spring when many of us are over here on the coast. We'd be safer in your company than the company a lot of us spend when we're not playing."

"I'll think about that and let you know. I think I could arrange that quickly enough. You boys may have a higher pot that I can play with now. I might have to throw my sports car into the pot. I might have to become one of that minivan kind of guys soon."

"You're fooling me?"

Drew shook his head and gave Phoebe a bit of a squeeze."

"Phoebe, how you have changed this man!"

"I'm starting to feel sorry about that, Cid," Phoebe said.

"Don't be. You're the best thing that happened to this guy! Look at him. He's gone from the big game with the boys. He moved on to be head of a company, took a year to live in France, and sampled all that wine and pasta. He doesn't have a sign of fat on him. I'm jealous! The man's got a perfect life!"

"But I can't be too sad. I'm in pretty good hands myself. If Rochelle hadn't agreed to us getting married, I would be a different man today."

Shortly afterward, they all walked back to the campsite. The friends grabbed a quick bite of breakfast before packing up. Goodbyes were said, and the friends separated with hugs and kisses.

Drew traveled down the dirt road until it met with the pavement. The interstate was easy to find from there. The lingering memories of salty beginnings were still in the air.

Phoebe recalled reading a book by Ali Howard when she was Drew's father was still a baby. She *wrote a passage.*

The salty beginnings were where the sea foam reaches its farthest inland point on the sandy beach. At this point, a new beginning of life begins never to be fully copied by any other specific grain of sand or drop of water. It is ours to watch and enjoy but to never keep to oneself.

On the way back to their home. Phoebe felt happy. She had stored the treasures in her mind. There was also satisfaction in being with those that meant so much to her and Drew. Yet, as they traveled further, she also began feeling sorrow. Phoebe felt a tinge of losing friends they had built over the past few months. Saying goodbye to friends was sad but natural. It was funny that she thought of the waves in New England in the winter on the ride home. She imagined the grayish shades of the water and how it smashed against the rocks. It brought a sense of God's divine plan. He was always in control.

Chapter 14

Holly Emmeline Taylor was born, causing tears of joy from both parents on Christmas Day later that year. Her parents were filled with gratitude, as one would expect with a Christmas child. Gifts came each day of the first-week baby Holly was home. Boxes and bags were stacked in the nursery until it was complete. The spare room was the next room to be filled with presents. There was an assortment of anything a child could need or want. There was no shortage of lambs, bears, and cuddly stuffed dogs.

Uncle Jesse took outstanding care of Socks, receiving lots of attention during this transition. He took it upon himself to adopt Socks during the first few weeks or longer. After that, the pug settled in well.

Drew ensured mother and child had all the comforts available. Phoebe was happy her mother offered to stay over the first two weeks after the baby came home so that Drew would be out of the house for several hours of the day.

Drew's hovering caused Phoebe to be afraid she would break out in hives. However, by the first week, Phoebe sent her home. Part of Phoebe's choice was selfish, as she wanted to be the one to bond with her baby first. Also, Phoebe wanted to prove to Drew that she could return to normal immediately. Drew had promised he would set up some time for her to meet with a recommended doctor in Atlanta and visit his old friend, Leo, whom Cid had mentioned.

Drew assured Phoebe he would arrange the meeting after the baby arrived and the doctor in Savannah cleared her for an exercise program. He wanted the absolute best for her.

Phoebe had been in total agreement. However, she dreamed of performing a pirouette once again. Phoebe's longing was to dance in the wind and to be in her husband's arms. She knew she had lost time since her injury. Cid had given her hope of repair her leg to a higher level of form and function. Phoebe knew she was being impatient, and her dream would come true in God's timing. In the meantime, she loved her family and appreciated each day with her husband and child.

By the third week home, Phoebe felt well enough to move freely around the house. Drew planned to be at the headquarters for only a half a day with only an hour from the house with traffic. He had no intentions of taking any overnight trips. However, being the man in charge did have some perks. Drew's mother was flying up at the end of the week, and she planned to help as much as Phoebe could. Drew suspected CeCe would be sent off on many muffin and coffee runs just so that Phoebe could have some time alone with the baby.

On Wednesday, the third week after Christmas day, the tide rolled ferociously in from a northeaster. Worse than the weather outside was the darkness that rolled into Drew's mind when he picked up the phone and heard Danny's voice.

"Drew, we need you at the ER. Shelly's at home with the baby, and they are fine. It's Phoebe. Something has happened to Phoebe."

Drew made it to the hospital by 3:05. Danny, Phoebe's parents, and Jesse, along with the hospital chaplain, awaited his arrival. Before Drew could get his bearings on what was happening, he was ushered into a conference room and asked to sit down. A few seconds later, a young physician no older than Phoebe walked into the room. Drew received the news that Phoebe had experienced a cerebral bleed in the brainstem. Unfortunately, she passed away at home before she made it to the local hospital's emergency room. Unfortunately, there wasn't anything the staff could do to save her. The hospital staff had her body in a private room to allow the family to say their goodbye. Plans to release the body for its preparation were awaiting Drew's de "I believe some of your family has stepped in to help facilitate the process. Everything awaits your wishes and any wishes your wife expressed in such a circumstance."

The family left together an hour later. Danny had taken the responsibility of watching over Drew.

As for Drew, his heart had left him the moment he walked into the room. and saw the stiff doll they said was his wife. That wasn't Phoebe in the bed with no movement. Phoebe was full of life. The photograph that he remembered of her from the pageant years ago showed a glow that called out to him. When he met her in the bakery, he knew he had found the sparkle that he had seen in that photo. She had the kind of life that lit the sky with stars. Now he felt the plunge of falling into the murky stormy sea of darkness.

Drew had been overwhelmed with grief with many of the steps involved. Drew and Phoebe's family stepped in to keep Drew's world afloat. The funeral passed, but the pain remained for all who knew Phoebe and loved her in many ways. Drew also had difficulty caring for Holly, so Danny and his wife stepped. They saw to it that Holly was loved and cared for, just as Phoebe would have wanted.

Drew walked around his daily life as a ghost for the first three months after Phoebe's passing. Friends stopped by to try to help, but all they met up with was a man in silence.

Cid took him out on the boat one afternoon to remove Drew from the places that reminded him of Phoebe. "Drew, you got to come out of this darkness. Holly needs you! We all need you back."

Drew's response was bleak. "I can't come out of this shell, Cid. It hurts too much to come out and see the sunshine again."

"Drew, Phoebe would not want you like this. Take what she gave you and run with it! Do you hear me? She gave you a play, and you have to run it. Pick up the love she gave you and get it down to the goal line. Otherwise, the opponent takes the ball and gets the point. Your team loses, buddy. That's the way it works. If you don't do your part, the whole team goes down. Are you going to let Holly be on the losing team? She's too young to play, so she has to sit on the bench for now. Your little girl is watching her Daddy. She needs you to get up off your keister and live. I'm not saying this to be mean. I'm saying this because people still need you to get in the game. We need our signal caller. She will not know how to pick up the football and rush 12 yards when things get tough."

"What are you talking about?" Drew asked with a snarl in his voice.

"I don't know. I want you to get off the bench and move the ball!" Cid said.

"I will think hard about what you said, Cid. Now for the remainder of the time until we are back on land, could you not say

another blessed word."

Cid gestured that he was zipping his lips to say no more and went about steering the boat.

Cid tied up the boat and secured it in the marina.

Drew grabbed Cid by the shoulders and cried with tears pouring down his cheeks. I don't want to let her go," he cried between sobs.

"I know, man."

"Thanks, Cid!" Drew said as he tried to get his composure. "I'm not going to sit on that cold bench anymore. I want to make sure of that. How mad would you have been if you had been there when Phoebe was attacked in Maine?"

"Do you even have to ask that?" Drew said with fury string to rise in voice and through his body.

"Then take that anger and dig yourself free, Drew. Phoebe would not leave you in that dark place you're in right now. She is out in the sunshine, dancing in the wind. So off that bench, Taylor! Your number is called!"

Drew took the meaning to heart that day. Eventually, he took to holding Holly again and investing his love in his daughter. Other changes occurred too. CeCe's husband decided to make some changes and retired from medicine in January following Phoebe's death. CeCe and her husband then sold their home and moved closer to Drew and their granddaughter. Holly was loved and cared for by her grandparents and extended family. Drew rarely went out of town, except on trips where Holly could travel with an entourage of people who cared for her needs. Drew watched his daughter grow up and fall in love with the sea. She had plenty of time to practice her dance on the beach and build her sandcastles with her cousins. As she reached her preschool years, it was clear that she would grow up to be a beauty like her mother.

In her third year, Drew took Holly to France with dotting grandparents and an entourage of staff. The cottage became a frolicking turmoil for the entire three weeks of December that

Drew spent with this family in a hamlet close to the country's northeastern border. He allowed the company employees to see Drew as a real human being, the way he was with his family during the three weeks in the village. He and Phoebe had experienced this exchange of mutual involvement when they had been in France five years earlier. It was a good lesson that his grandfather had taught him about doing business and about living life.

In Holly's fourth year, she attracted her first boyfriend at the international preschool where she was enrolled. Drew had become suspicious of the little guy when the friendly classmate wanted to carry her bookbag and put it in the cubby when she walked into her class each morning. Drew breathed easier when this suitor moved with his parents to Denver during the Fall break.

Grandpa Farmer reassured Drew that it was okay for a little bit of preferential friendship at this age. "Phoebe had her beaus starting at about four. However, she did have her brother, Danny, to keep her out of trouble. The twins told us everything about each other so we could douse the flame quickly if we thought things were moving too fast, and we never worried. We decided in high school that one of Phoebe's parents was always with her when she was out with friends. She may have hated it, but her mother and I could sleep at night."

Drew learned to appreciate the wisdom of the quiet man who teased unmercifully and could address any technology programming concern one might face. Behind glasses and graying hair was a man who loved his family and made choices to express that love regularly.

On her fifth birthday, Drew and got up early. Holly had spent the night with her grandparents. He was alone, so he headed for the beach area in front of Phoebe's cottage, where she lived when they first met. The wind was nippy coming off the Atlantic in December. Drew felt the stinging breeze and sand pelting against his skin. It felt good as it let him know that he was still alive. The grit on his skin felt rough on his cheeks. Suddenly he smelled a floral scent. He thought he heard a whisper.

"I've been calling you."

He listened closer, but all he heard was the whistling of the wind. Drew closed his eyes and hoped he would hear it again. But instead, he started walking again, and this time he heard laughter from a bluff on his left. The shimmer from the water blinded him for a second, even though Drew was wearing sunglasses. He turned his head away, hoping to adjust his eyes to the brightness. Drew glanced, and for a moment, a young man and a woman appeared standing on the bluff laughing. For instance, he saw himself holding Phoebe as she looked out towards the sea with her toes and shoes pointed downward, grazing the sand. Drew could almost experience the touch of his hands as he felt the warmth from the body come through the fabric as she danced in his arms.

Drew tried to listen to what they were saying. Suddenly he heard a voice he knew that brought him to the present.

"Daddy, here I am!" a young voice was calling out in the wind. She started running through the sand toward Drew.

He looked down at the beach at a young girl, waving her hands and moving toward him quickly. "Happy birthday, sweetheart!" He raided out his arms and began running toward the child. I missed you very much this morning, so I came out early so I wouldn't wake up your grandparents before I came to pick you up."

"Grandma said she thought you might be out here taking a morning walk. I begged her to let me get you. Grandma and Grandpa Farmer called and said they had blueberry and cinnamon muffins hot from the oven. Uncle Danny said the chocolate cakes with icing were your favorite. He told me if you don't come over now, he'd eat the one left for you."

"I bet he would too!"

"Daddy?" Holly looked up at her father with her innocent eyes.

"Yes." Drew looked down at his daughter, wondering what was on her mind.

"Did you see Mommy today?"

Drew took a deep breath and answered her question honestly, as a five-year-old would understand. "Sweetheart, I see your mother every day in every star, rainbow, and light shimmer. Your mother taught me to see her reflection in everything that was and is beautiful. That's why I see so much of her in you! She wants us to be free to live, love, and laugh, and that's want I want to find again."

"That's what I want you to look for every day." responded the child's father.

Drew and Holly met up with Drew's family, and they made it back to their cars. It was time to celebrate Holly's growing up. She was the next generation. But Drew wanted to continue sharing the gift he learned he had in his heart for all things made of God and love.

Other Books by D.L. Barnes

Other books in the Coastal Saga series:

Salty Beginnings

Burning Bush Bakery

Captain Bodacious

About the Author

D.L. Barnes lives near the north Georgia mountains. The natural beauty of the Georgia and Carolina coast inspired the Coastal Saga series.

www.ingramcontent.com/pod-product-compliance
Lightning Source LLC
LaVergne TN
LVHW050630100826
845148LV00011B/1815

* 9 7 9 8 9 8 6 7 0 1 9 5 0 *